Entire contents © 2015 Anouk Ricard. Translation © 2015 Helge Dascher. Translation editor: John Kadlecek. All rights reserved. No part of this book (except small portions for review purposes) may be reproduced in any form without written permission from Anouk Ricard or Enfant. Enfant is an imprint of Drawn & Quarterly. Originally published in French as *Anna et Froga: Top Niveau* by Éditions Sarbacane. First hardcover edition: October 2015. 10 9 8 7 6 5 4 3 2 1. Printed in Malaysia. Library and Archives Canada Cataloguing in Publication: Ricard, Anouk [*Top niveau*. English] *Fore!* / Anouk Ricard ; [translator, Helge Dascher]. (*Anna and Froga*). Translation of: *Anna et Froga: top niveau*. ISBN 978-1-77046-204-5 (bound) 1. Graphic novels. I. Dascher, Helge, 1965-, translator II. Title. III. Title: Top niveau. English. IV. Series: Ricard, Anouk. Anna et Froga. English.PZ7.7.R53F67 2015 j741.5'944 C2014-907027-6. This work, published as part of

Liberté • Égalité • Fraternité
RÉPUBLIQUE FRANÇAISE

grant programs for publication (Acquisition of Rights and Translation), received support from the French Ministry of Foreign and European Affairs and from the Institut français. Cet ouvrage, publié dans le cadre du Programme d'Aide à la Publication (Cession de droits et Traduction), a bénéficié du soutien du Ministère des Affaires étrangères et européennes et de l'Institut français. Drawn & Quarterly acknowledges the financial support of the Government of Canada through the Canada Book Fund, the Canada Council for the Arts, and the National Translation Program for Book Publishing, an initiative of the *Roadmap for Canada's Official Languages 2013–2018: Education, Immigration, Communities,* for our translation activities. Published in the USA by Drawn & Quarterly, a client publisher of Farrar, Straus and Giroux. Orders: 888.330.8477. Published in Canada by Drawn & Quarterly, a client publisher of Raincoast Books. Orders: 800.663.5714. Published in the United Kingdom by Drawn & Quarterly, a client publisher of Publishers Group UK. Orders: info@pguk.co.uk.

Anouk Ricard

ANNA & FROGA

Fore!

ENFANT

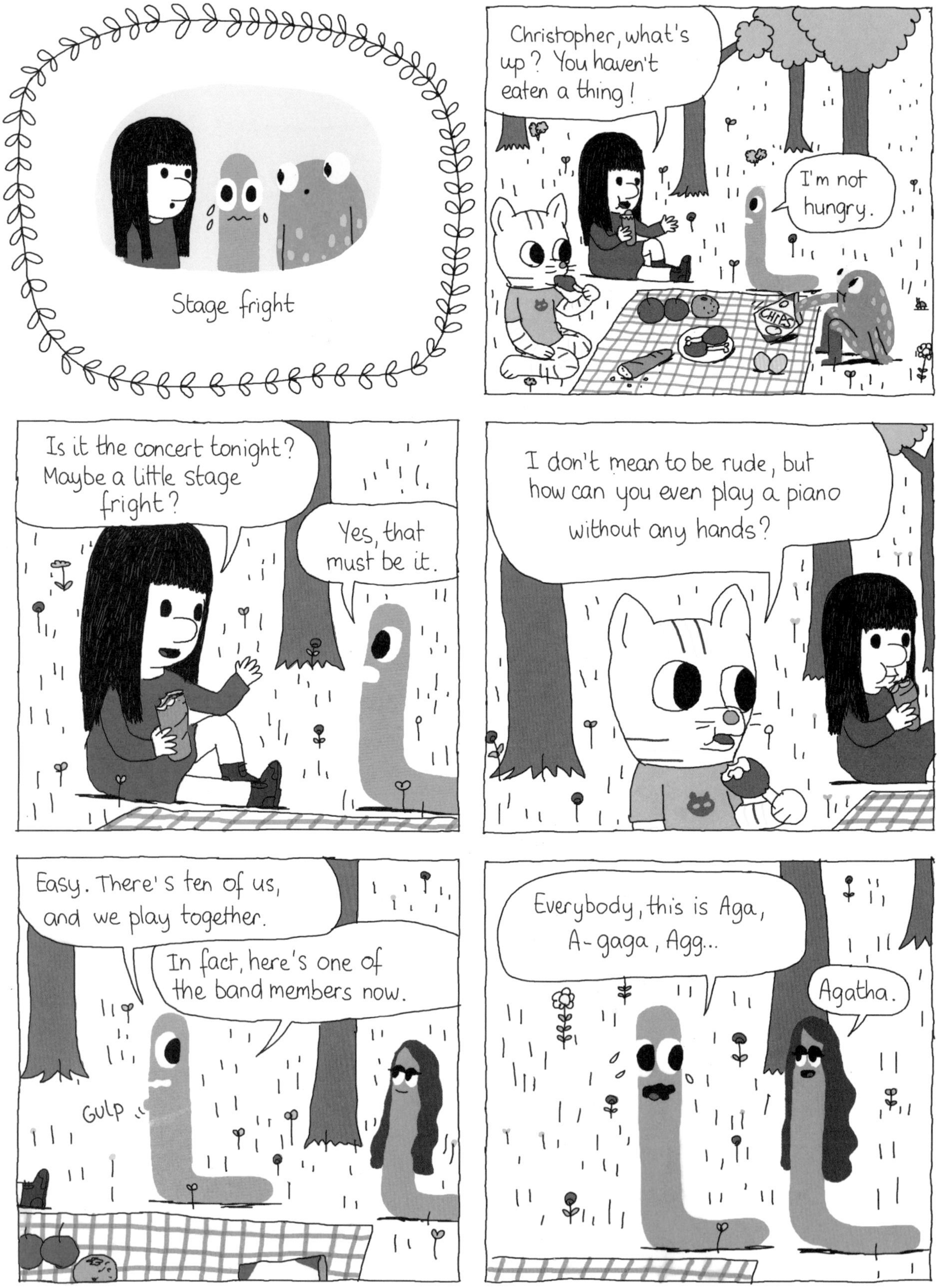
Stage fright
Christopher, what's up? You haven't eaten a thing!
CHIPS
I'm not hungry.
Is it the concert tonight? Maybe a little stage fright?
Yes, that must be it.
I don't mean to be rude, but how can you even play a piano without any hands?
Easy. There's ten of us, and we play together.
In fact, here's one of the band members now.
GULP
Everybody, this is Aga, A-gaga, Agg..
Agatha.

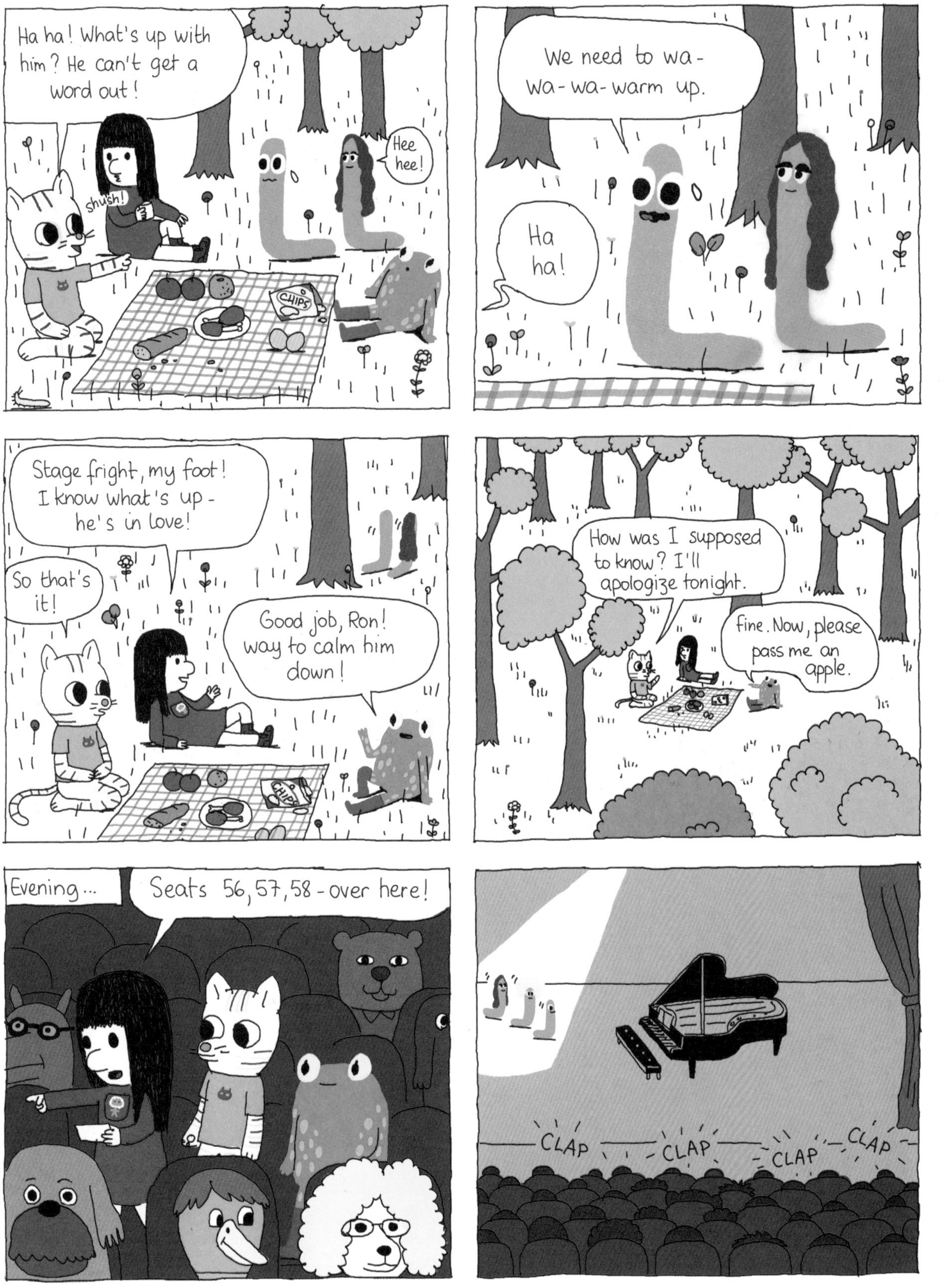
Ha ha! What's up with him? He can't get a word out!
Hee hee!
shush!
CHIPS
We need to wa-wa-wa-warm up.
Ha ha!
Stage fright, my foot! I know what's up - he's in love!
So that's it!
Good job, Ron! Way to calm him down!
CHIPS
How was I supposed to know? I'll apologize tonight.
Fine. Now, please pass me an apple.
Evening...
Seats 56, 57, 58 - over here!
CLAP
CLAP
CLAP
CLAP

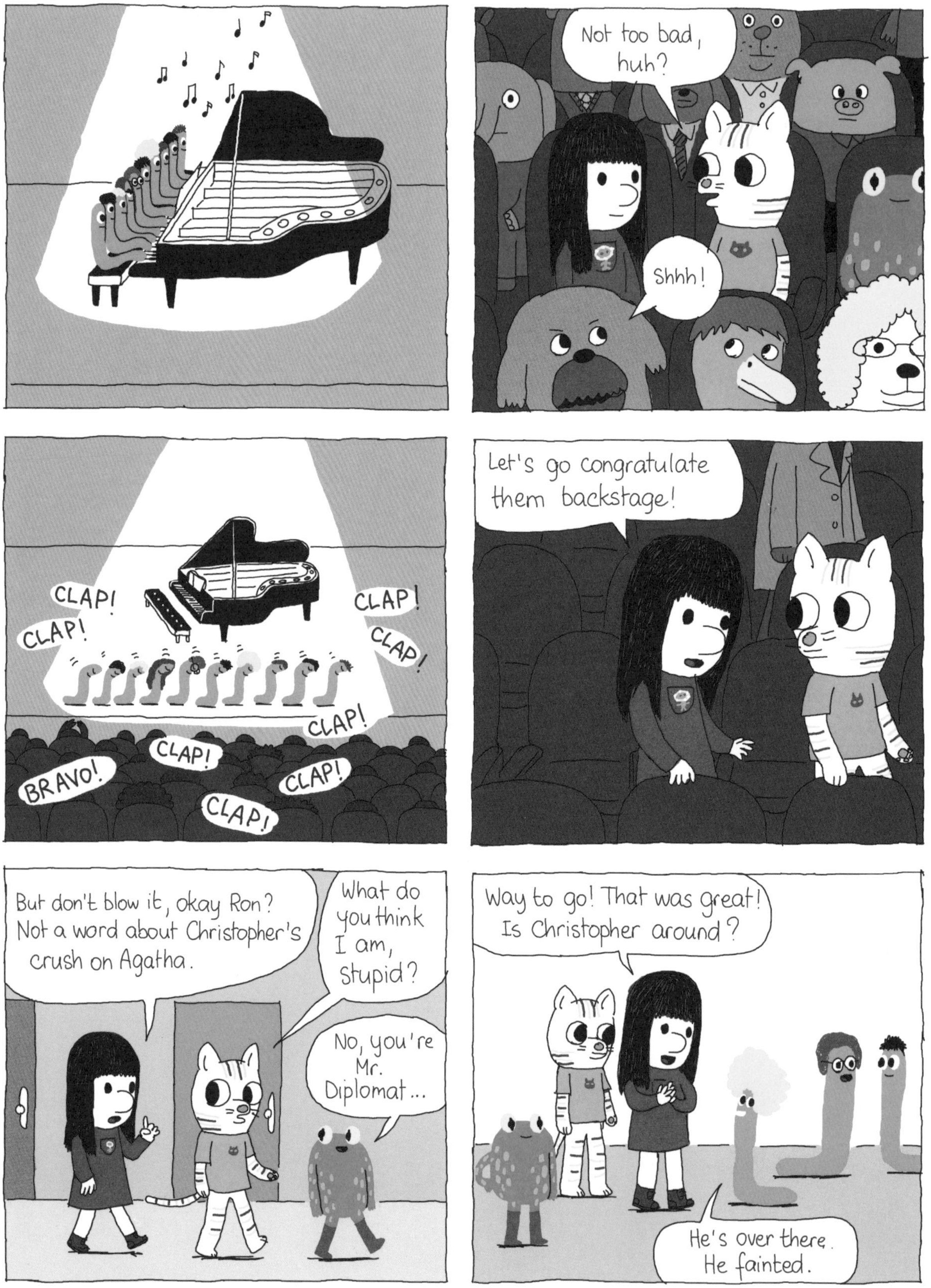
Not too bad, huh?
Shhh!
CLAP!
CLAP!
CLAP!
CLAP!
CLAP!
CLAP!
BRAVO!
CLAP!
CLAP!
Let's go congratulate them backstage!
But don't blow it, okay Ron? Not a word about Christopher's crush on Agatha.
What do you think I am, stupid?
No, you're Mr. Diplomat...
Way to go! That was great! Is Christopher around?
He's over there. He fainted.

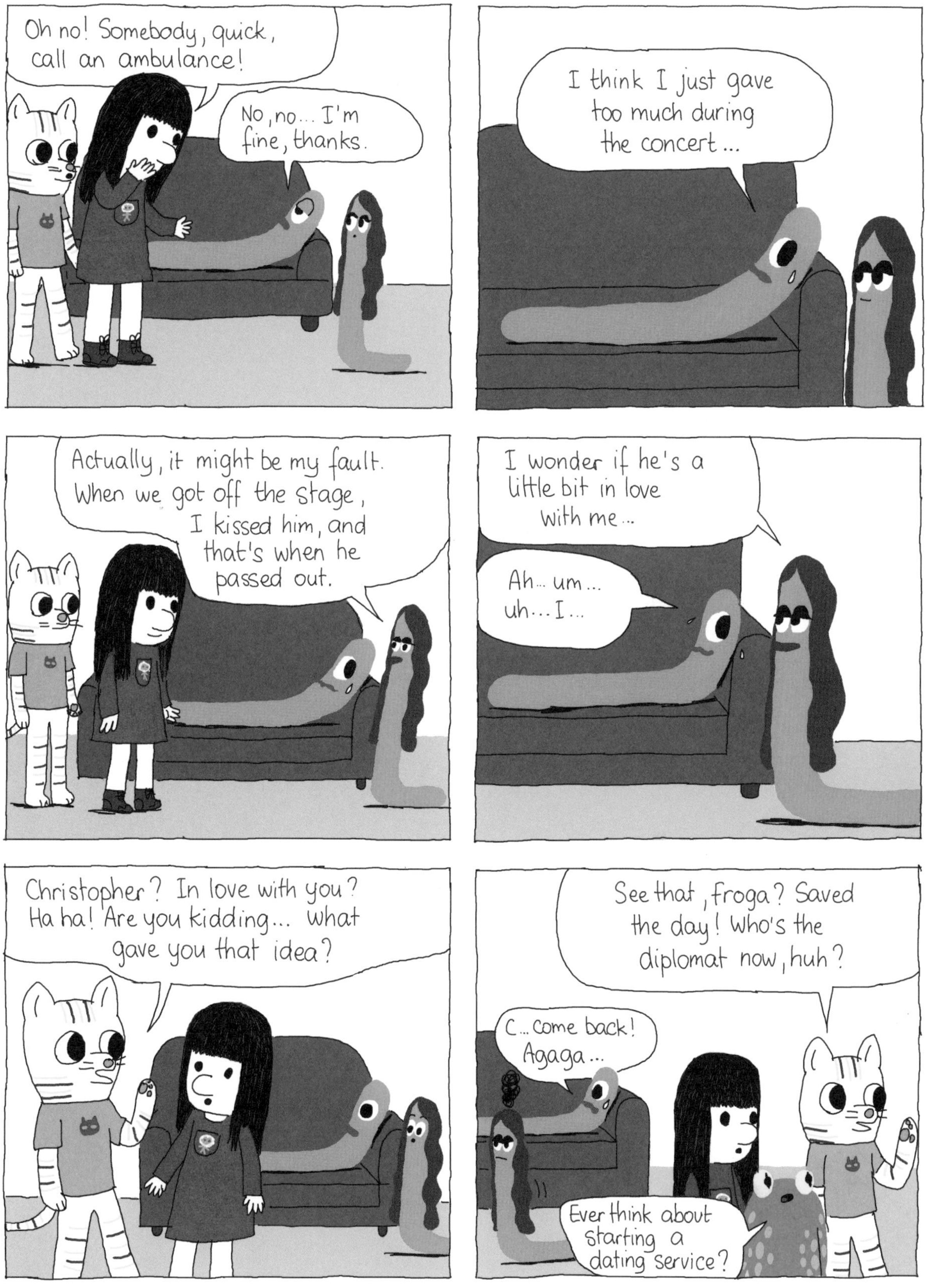
Oh no! Somebody, quick, call an ambulance!
No, no... I'm fine, thanks.
I think I just gave too much during the concert...
Actually, it might be my fault. When we got off the stage, I kissed him, and that's when he passed out.
I wonder if he's a little bit in love with me...
Ah... um... uh... I...
Christopher? In love with you? Ha ha! Are you kidding... what gave you that idea?
See that, Froga? Saved the day! Who's the diplomat now, huh?
C... come back! Agaga...
Ever think about starting a dating service?

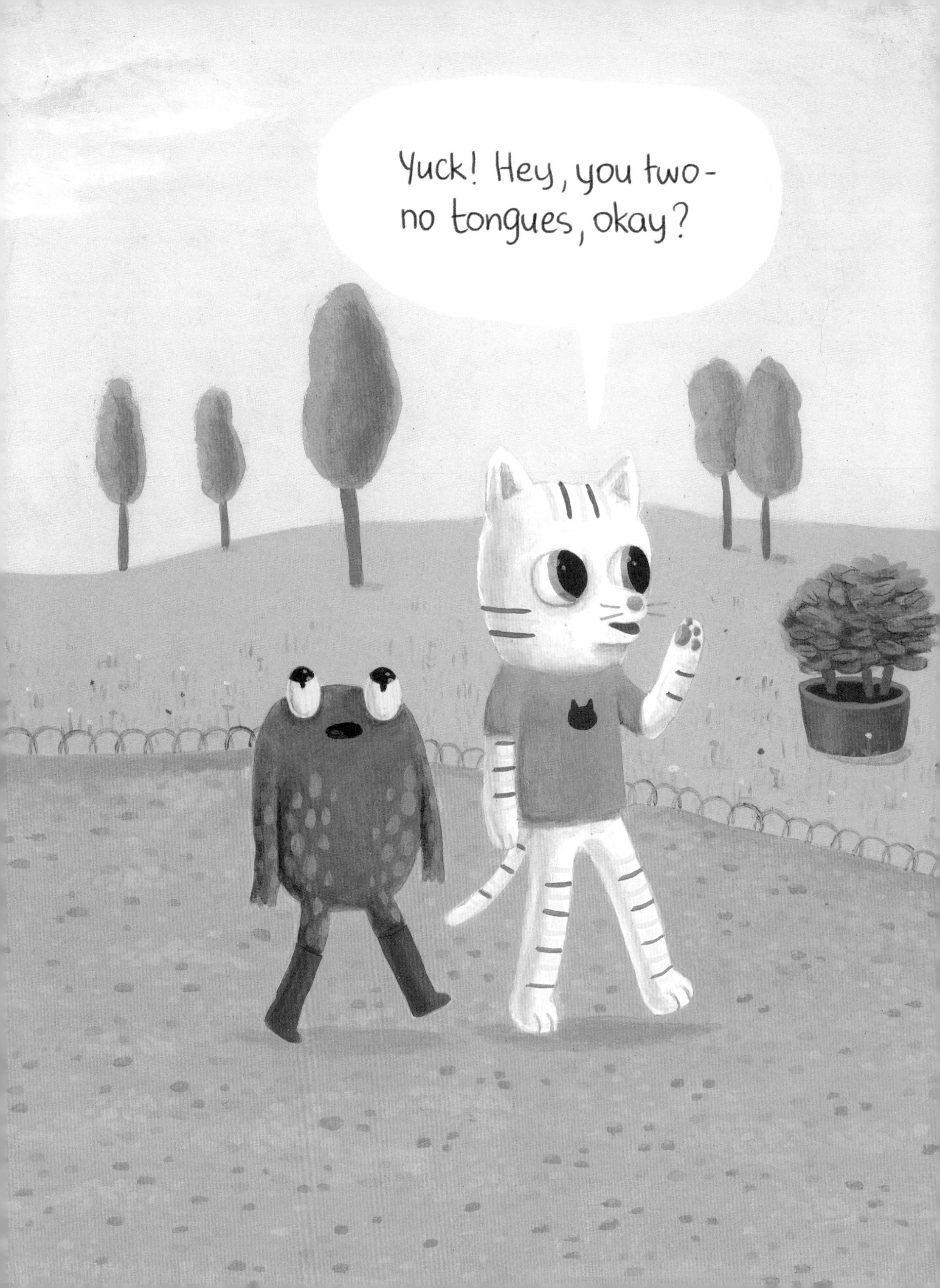
Yuck! Hey, you two- no tongues, okay?

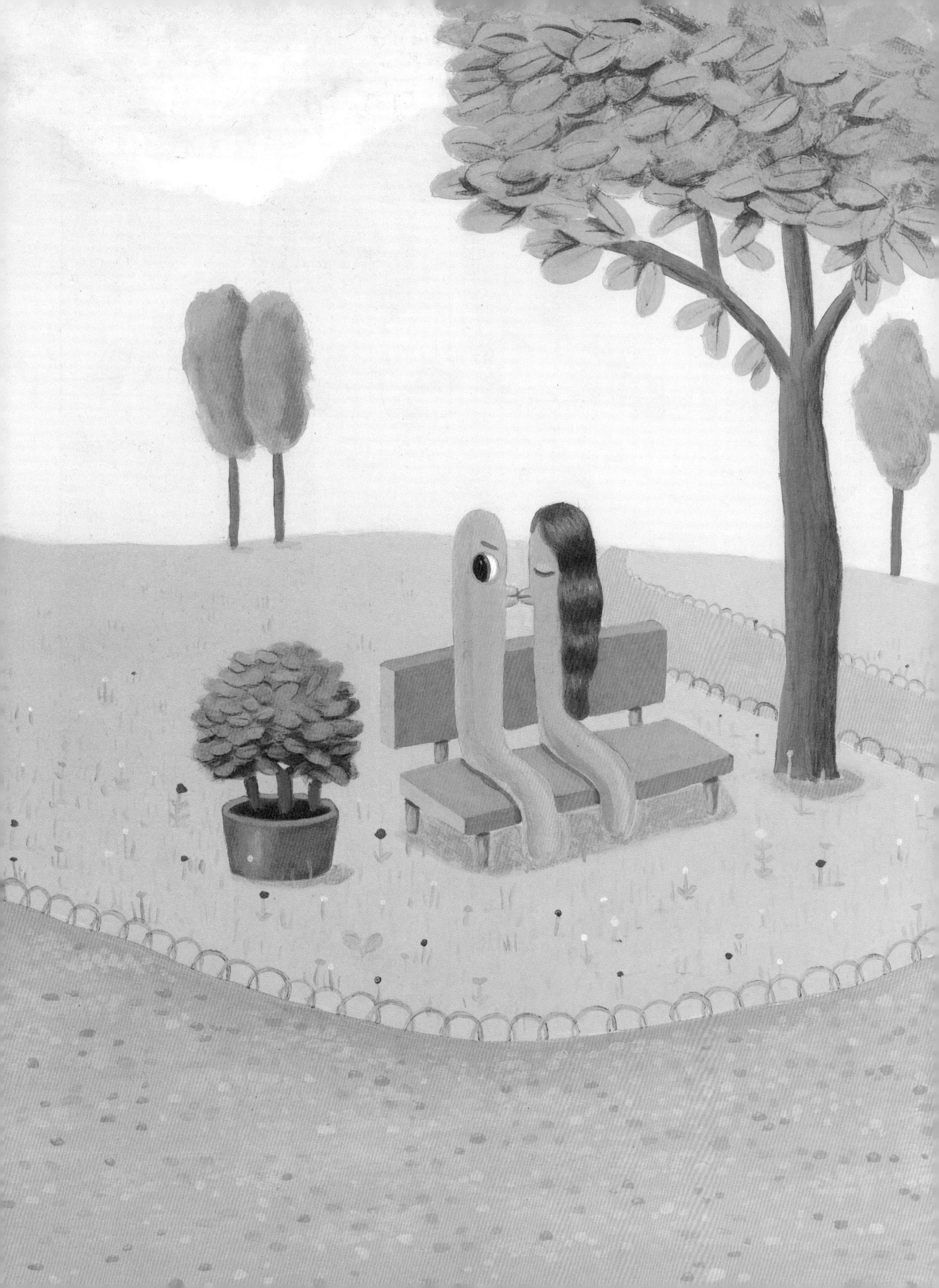

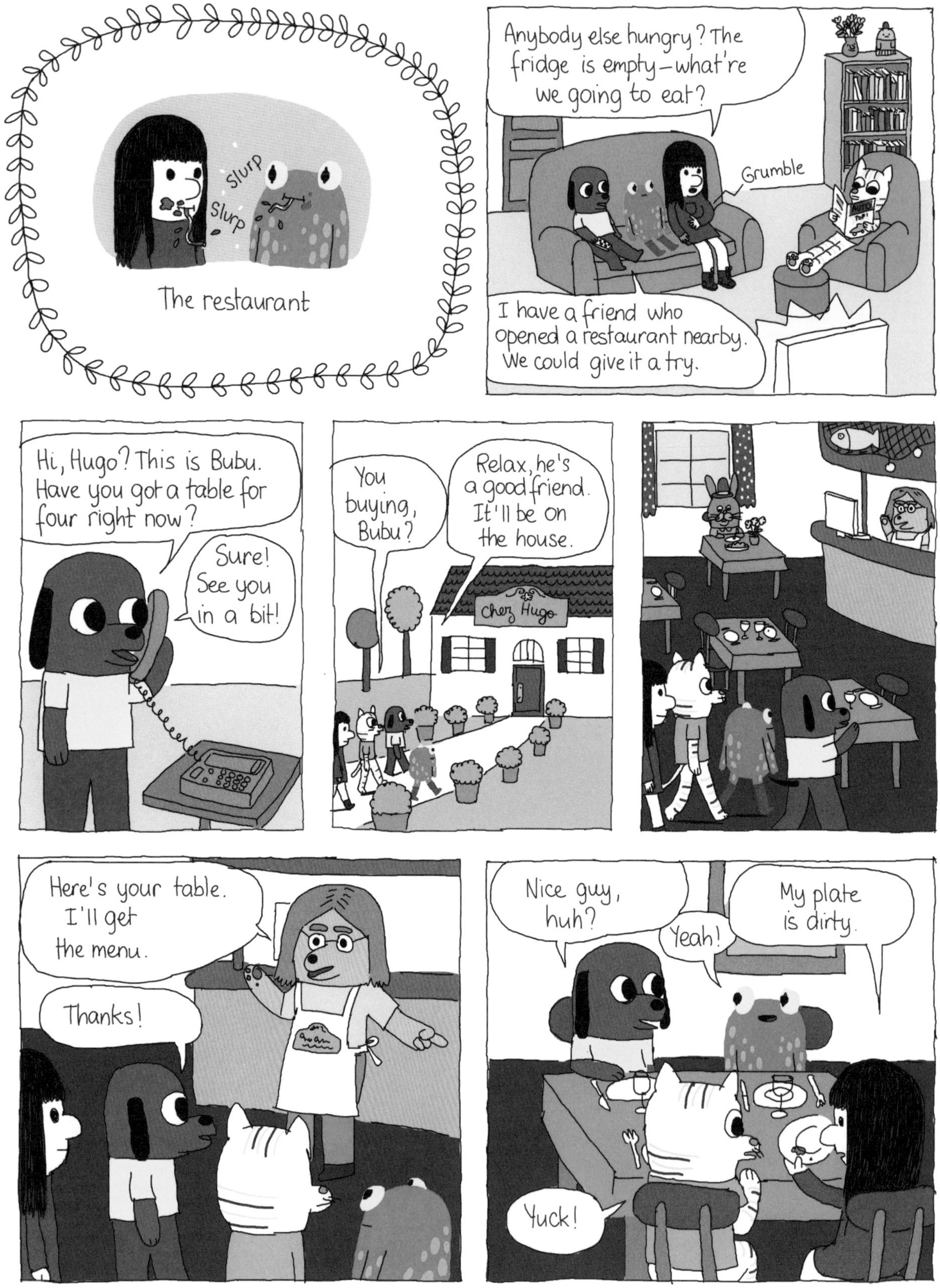
Slurp
Slurp
The restaurant
Anybody else hungry? The fridge is empty—what're we going to eat?
Grumble
I have a friend who opened a restaurant nearby. We could give it a try.
Hi, Hugo? This is Bubu. Have you got a table for four right now?
Sure! See you in a bit!
You buying, Bubu?
Relax, he's a good friend. It'll be on the house.
Chez Hugo
Here's your table. I'll get the menu.
Thanks!
Nice guy, huh?
Yeah!
My plate is dirty.
Yuck!

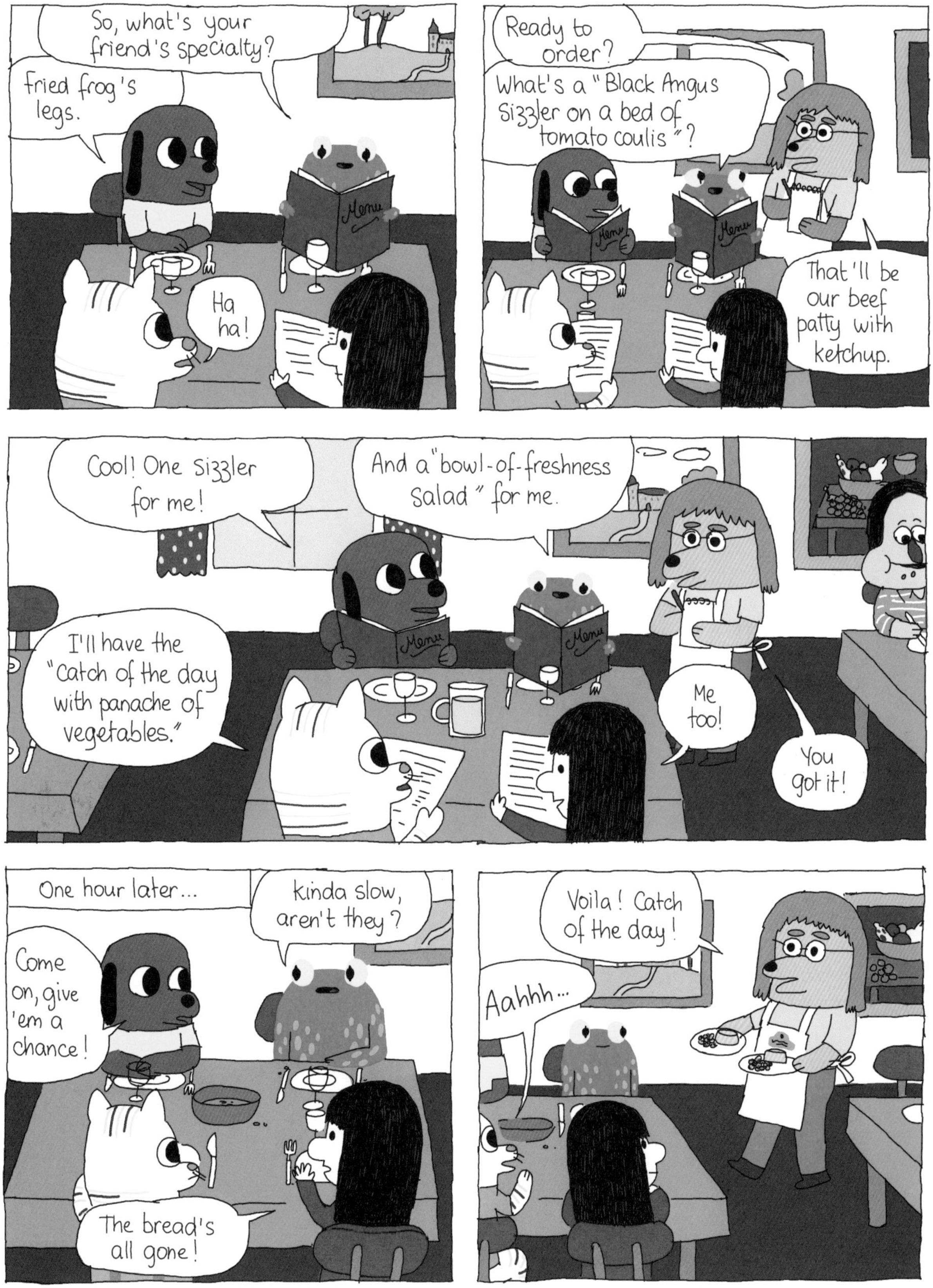
So, what's your friend's specialty?
fried frog's legs.
Ha ha!
Ready to order?
What's a "Black Angus Sizzler on a bed of tomato coulis"?
That'll be our beef patty with ketchup.
Cool! One Sizzler for me!
And a "bowl-of-freshness salad" for me.
I'll have the "catch of the day with panache of vegetables."
Me too!
You got it!
One hour later...
Kinda slow, aren't they?
Come on, give 'em a chance!
The bread's all gone!
Voila! Catch of the day!
Aahhh...

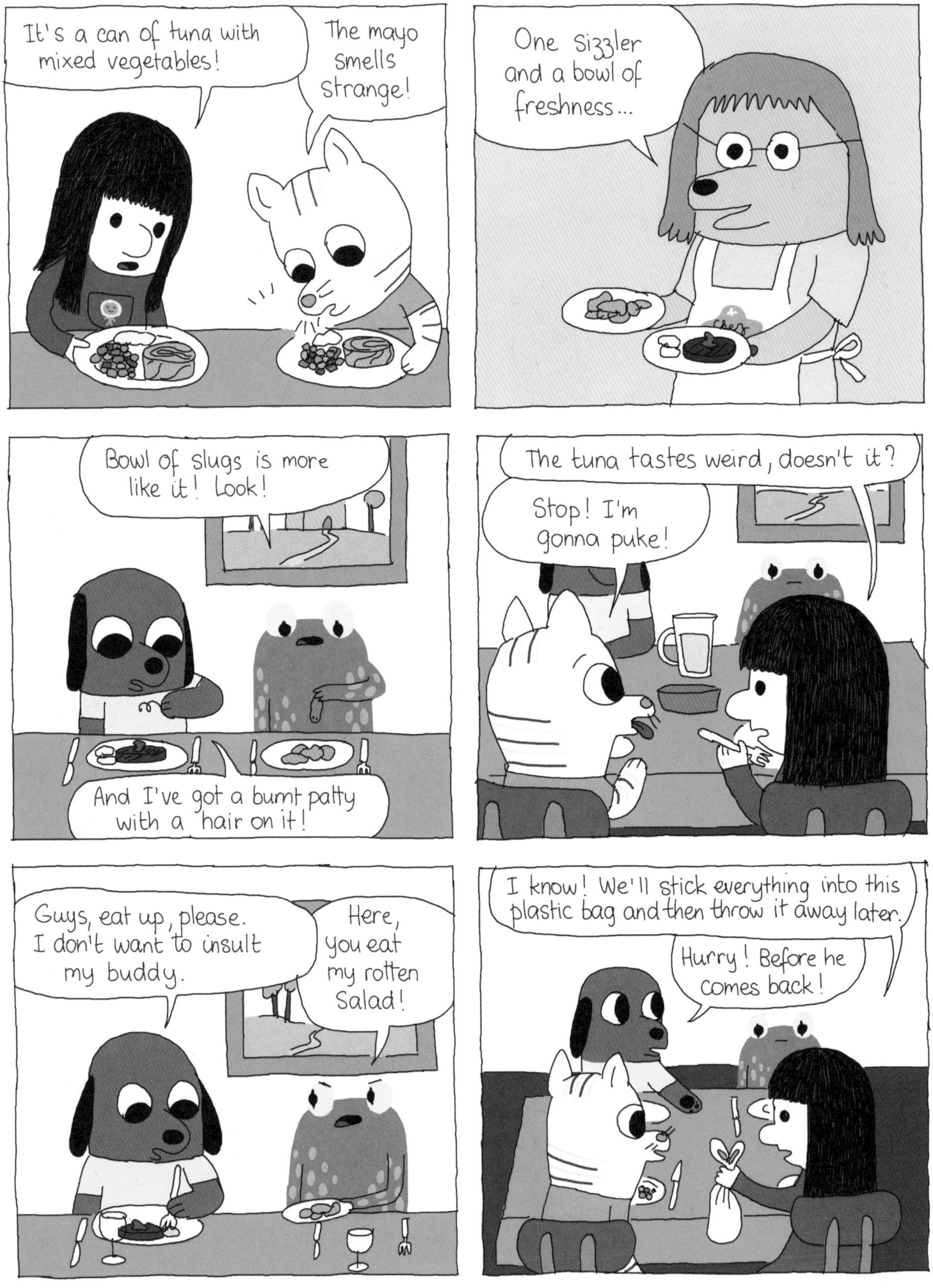
It's a can of tuna with mixed vegetables!
The mayo smells strange!
One Sizzler and a bowl of freshness...
Bowl of slugs is more like it! Look!
And I've got a burnt patty with a hair on it!
The tuna tastes weird, doesn't it?
Stop! I'm gonna puke!
Guys, eat up, please. I don't want to insult my buddy.
Here, you eat my rotten Salad!
I know! We'll stick everything into this plastic bag and then throw it away later.
Hurry! Before he comes back!

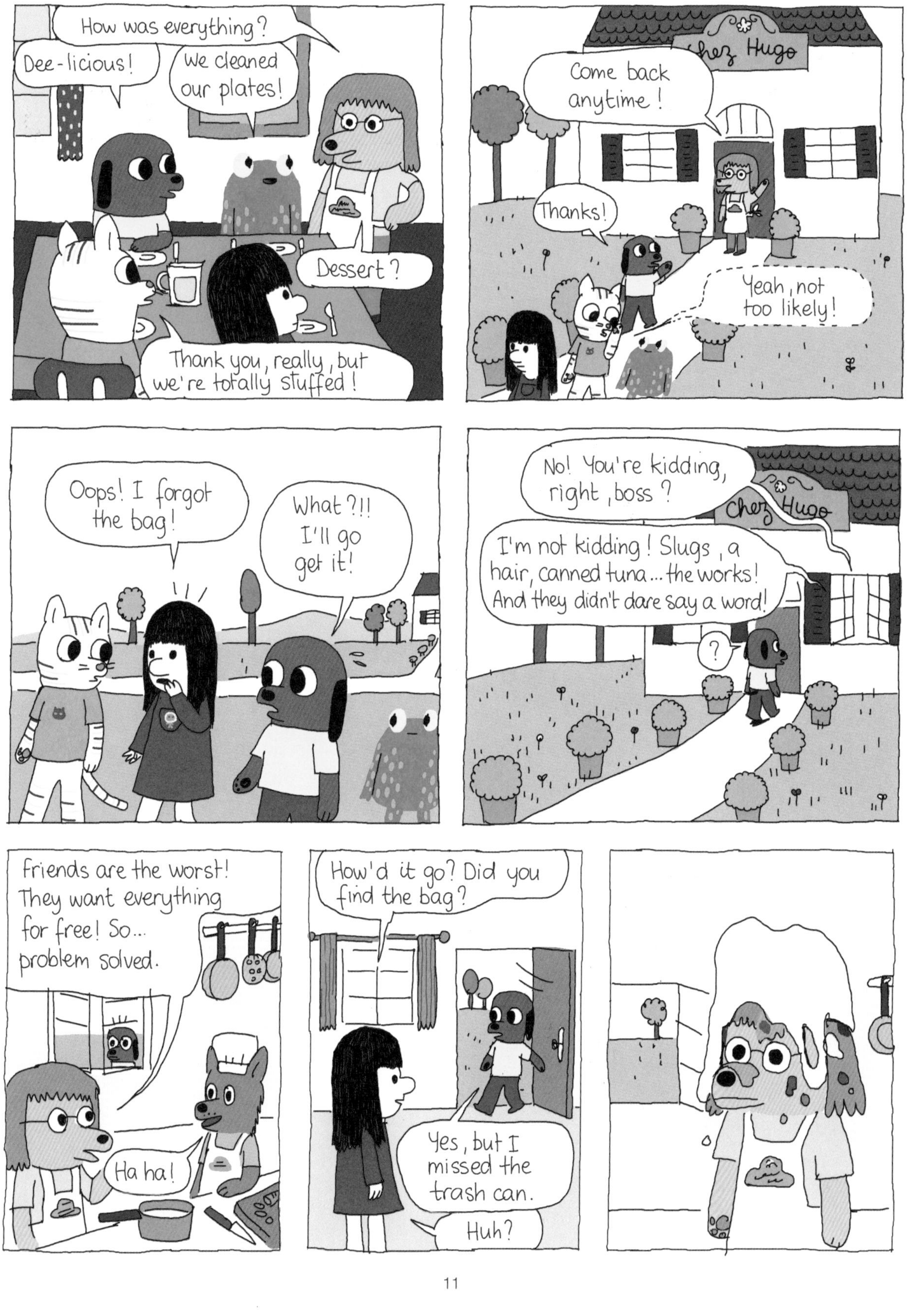
How was everything?
Dee-licious!
We cleaned our plates!
Dessert?
Thank you, really, but we're totally stuffed!
Chez Hugo
Come back anytime!
Thanks!
Yeah, not too likely!
Oops! I forgot the bag!
What?!! I'll go get it!
No! You're kidding, right, boss?
Chez Hugo
I'm not kidding! Slugs, a hair, canned tuna... the works! And they didn't dare say a word!
?
Friends are the worst! They want everything for free! So... problem solved.
Ha ha!
How'd it go? Did you find the bag?
Yes, but I missed the trash can.
Huh?

Cooking with Bubu

Okay, who wants to learn how to cook my famous "Pasta alla Bubu"?

Not me.

Sure you do! You'll see. First, you boil up some noodles.

Makes sense.

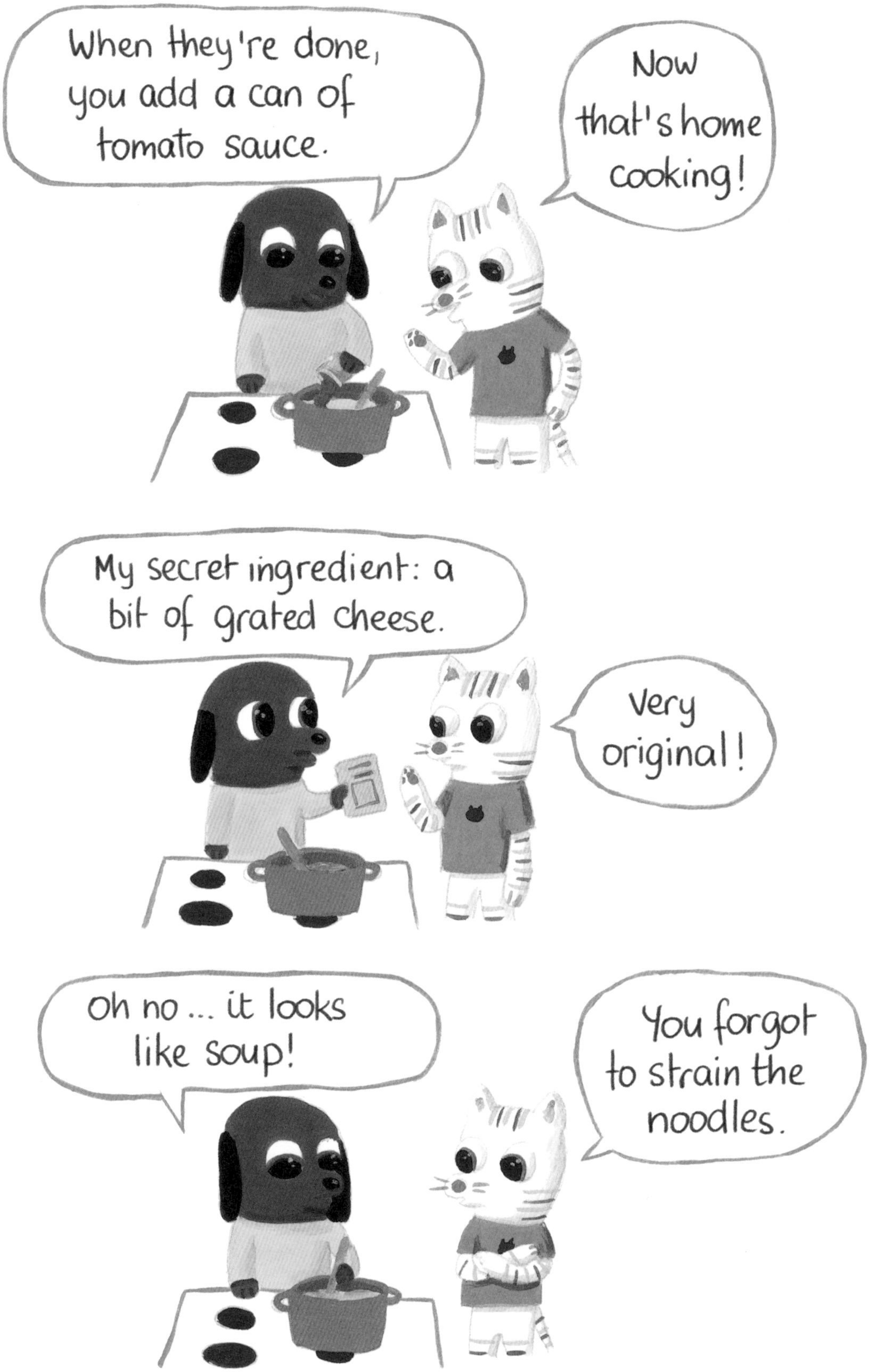
When they're done, you add a can of tomato sauce.
Now that's home cooking!
My secret ingredient: a bit of grated cheese.
Very original!
Oh no ... it looks like soup!
You forgot to strain the noodles.

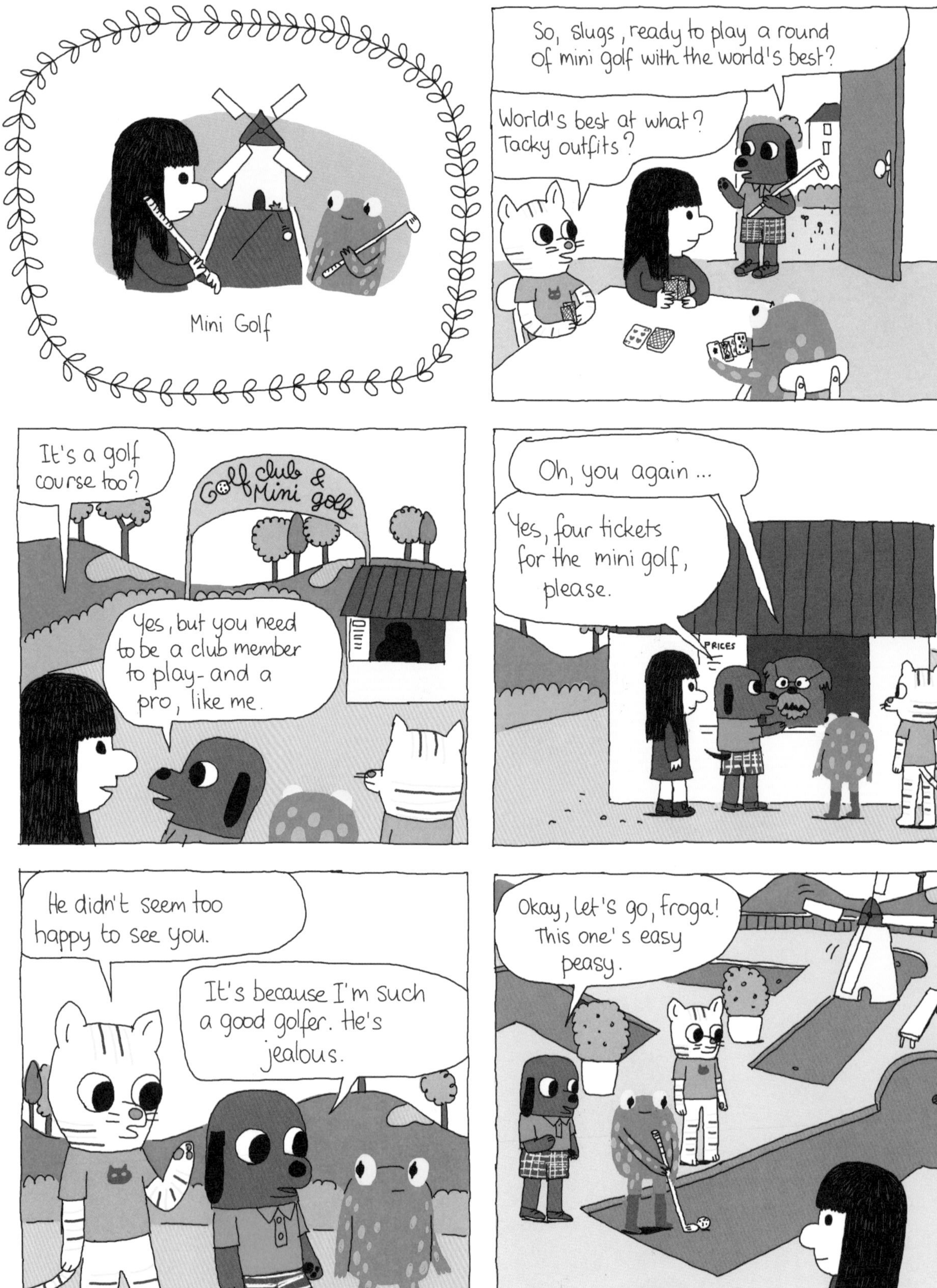
Mini Golf
So, slugs, ready to play a round of mini golf with the world's best?
World's best at what? Tacky outfits?
It's a golf course too?
Golf club & Mini golf
Yes, but you need to be a club member to play - and a pro, like me.
Oh, you again ...
Yes, four tickets for the mini golf, please.
PRICES
He didn't seem too happy to see you.
It's because I'm such a good golfer. He's jealous.
Okay, let's go, froga! This one's easy peasy.

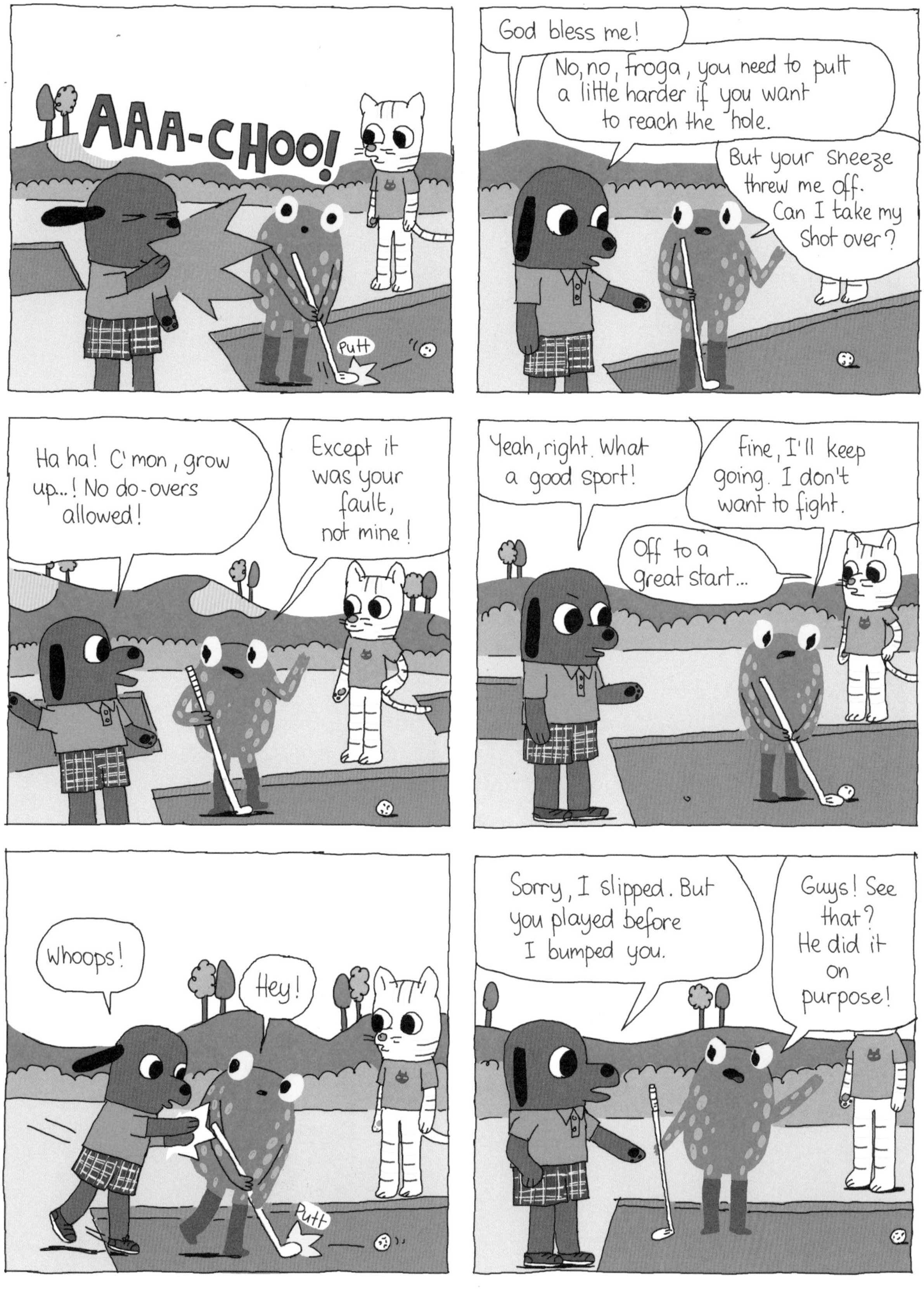
AAA-CHOO!
Putt
God bless me!
No, no, froga, you need to putt a little harder if you want to reach the hole.
But your sneeze threw me off. Can I take my shot over?
Ha ha! C'mon, grow up...! No do-overs allowed!
Except it was your fault, not mine!
Yeah, right. What a good sport!
Fine, I'll keep going. I don't want to fight.
Off to a great start...
Whoops!
Hey!
Putt
Sorry, I slipped. But you played before I bumped you.
Guys! See that? He did it on purpose!

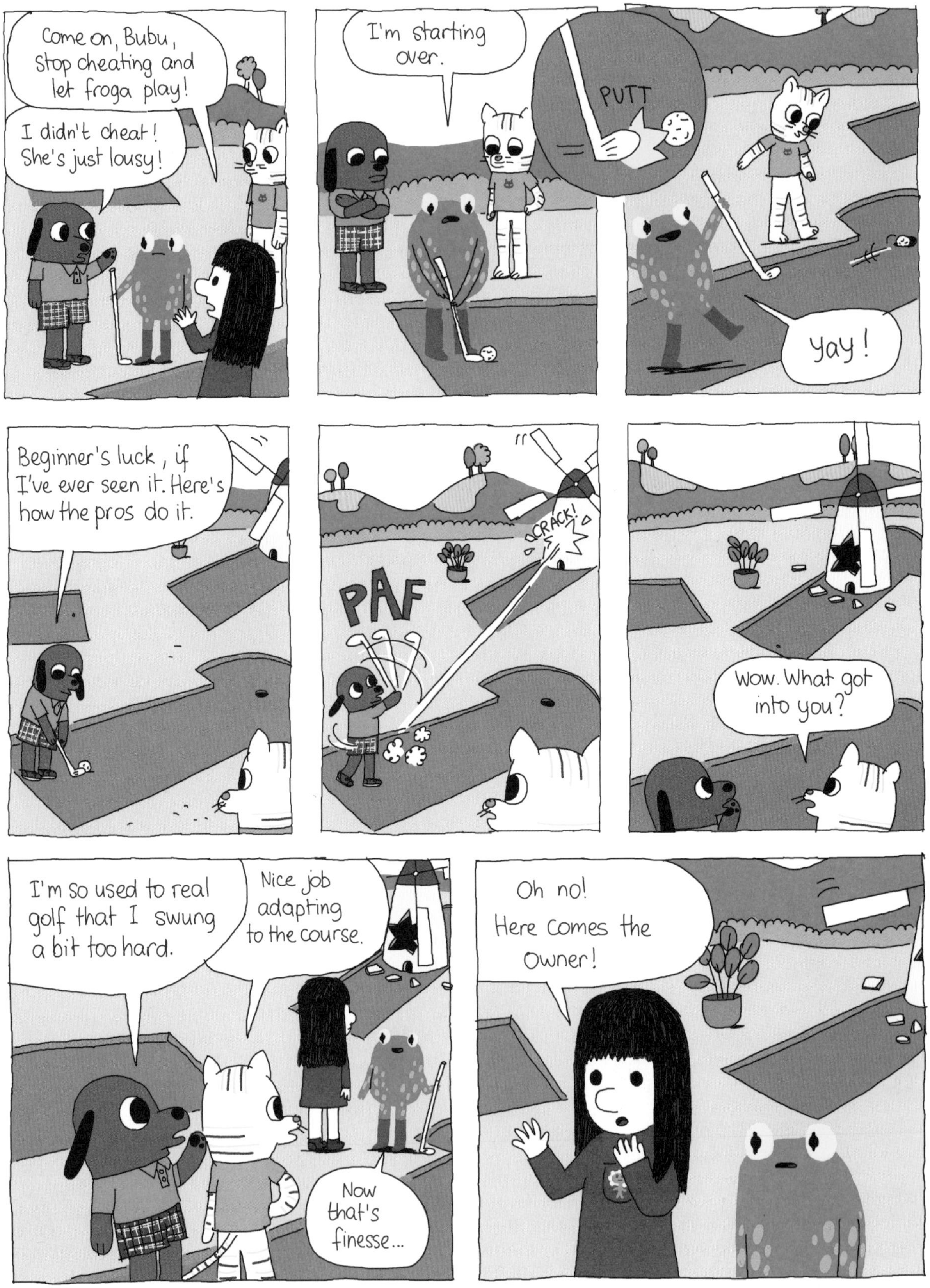

Come on, Bubu, Stop cheating and let froga play!
I didn't cheat! She's just lousy!
I'm starting over.
PUTT
Yay!
Beginner's luck, if I've ever seen it. Here's how the pros do it.
PAF
CRACK!
Wow. What got into you?
I'm so used to real golf that I swung a bit too hard.
Nice job adapting to the course.
Now that's finesse...
Oh no! Here comes the Owner!

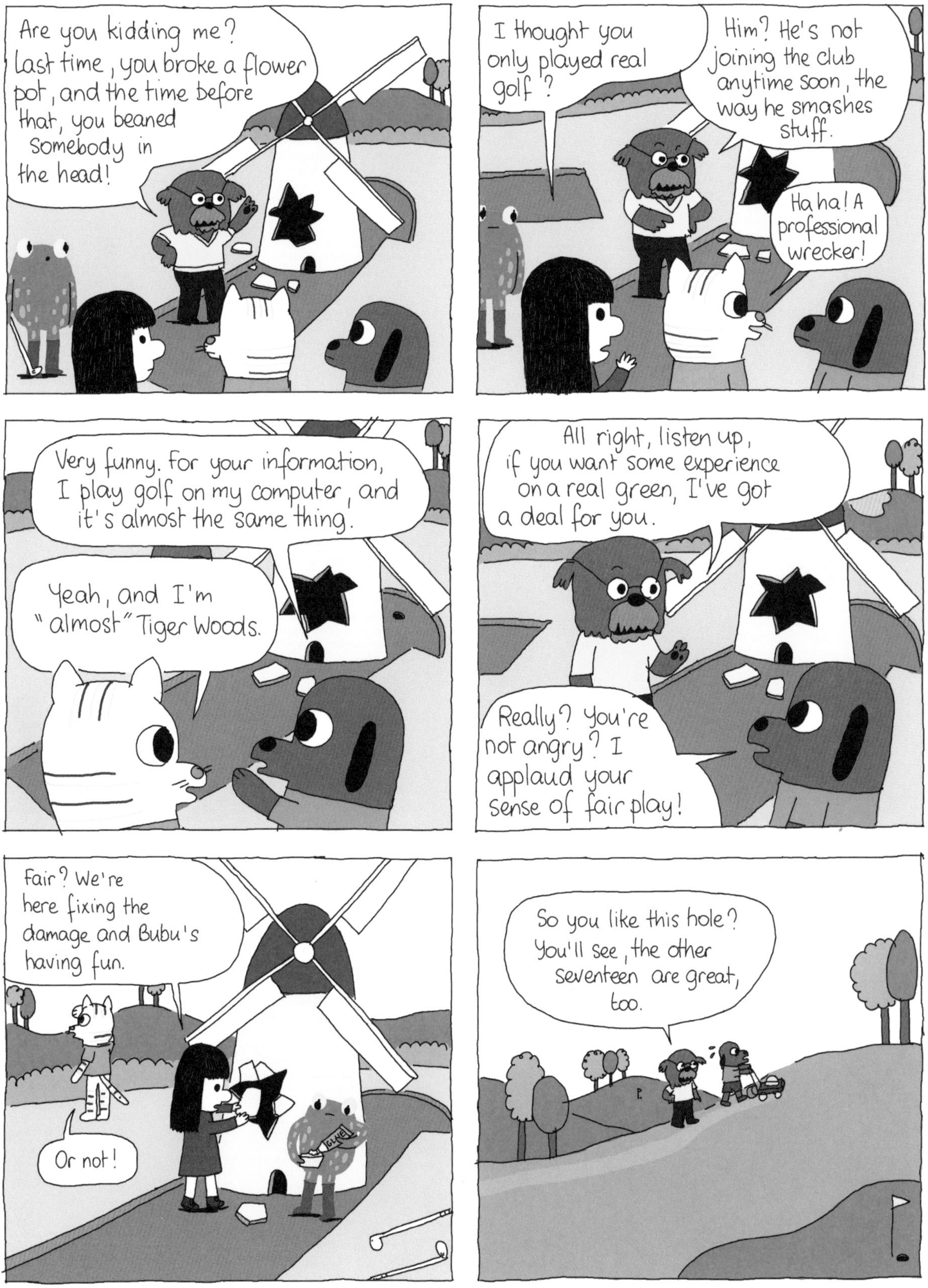
Are you kidding me? Last time, you broke a flower pot, and the time before that, you beaned somebody in the head!
I thought you only played real golf?
Him? He's not joining the club anytime soon, the way he smashes stuff.
Ha ha! A professional wrecker!
Very funny. For your information, I play golf on my computer, and it's almost the same thing.
Yeah, and I'm "almost" Tiger Woods.
All right, listen up, if you want some experience on a real green, I've got a deal for you.
Really? You're not angry? I applaud your sense of fair play!
Fair? We're here fixing the damage and Bubu's having fun.
Or not!
GLUE
So you like this hole? You'll see, the other seventeen are great, too.

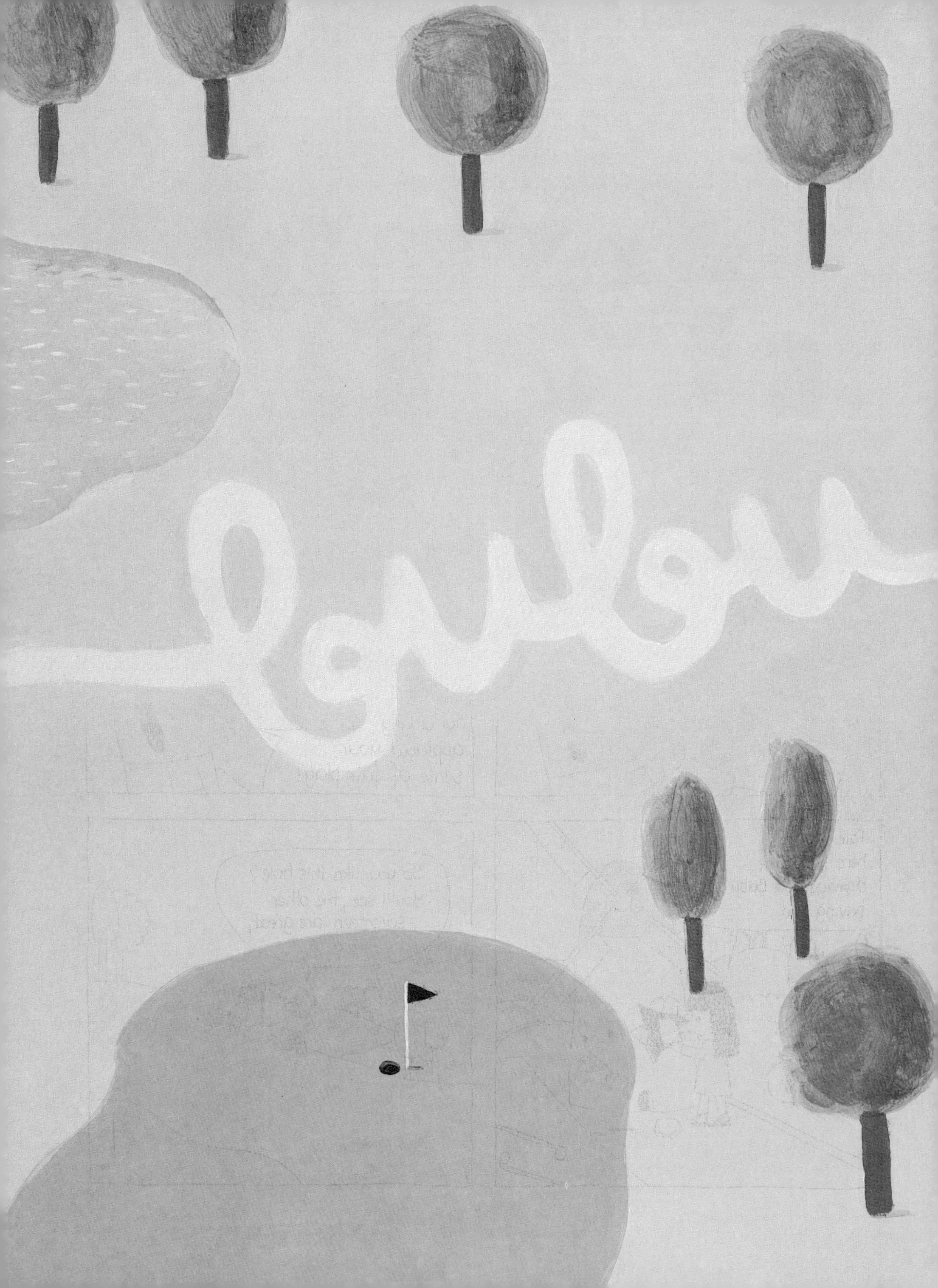

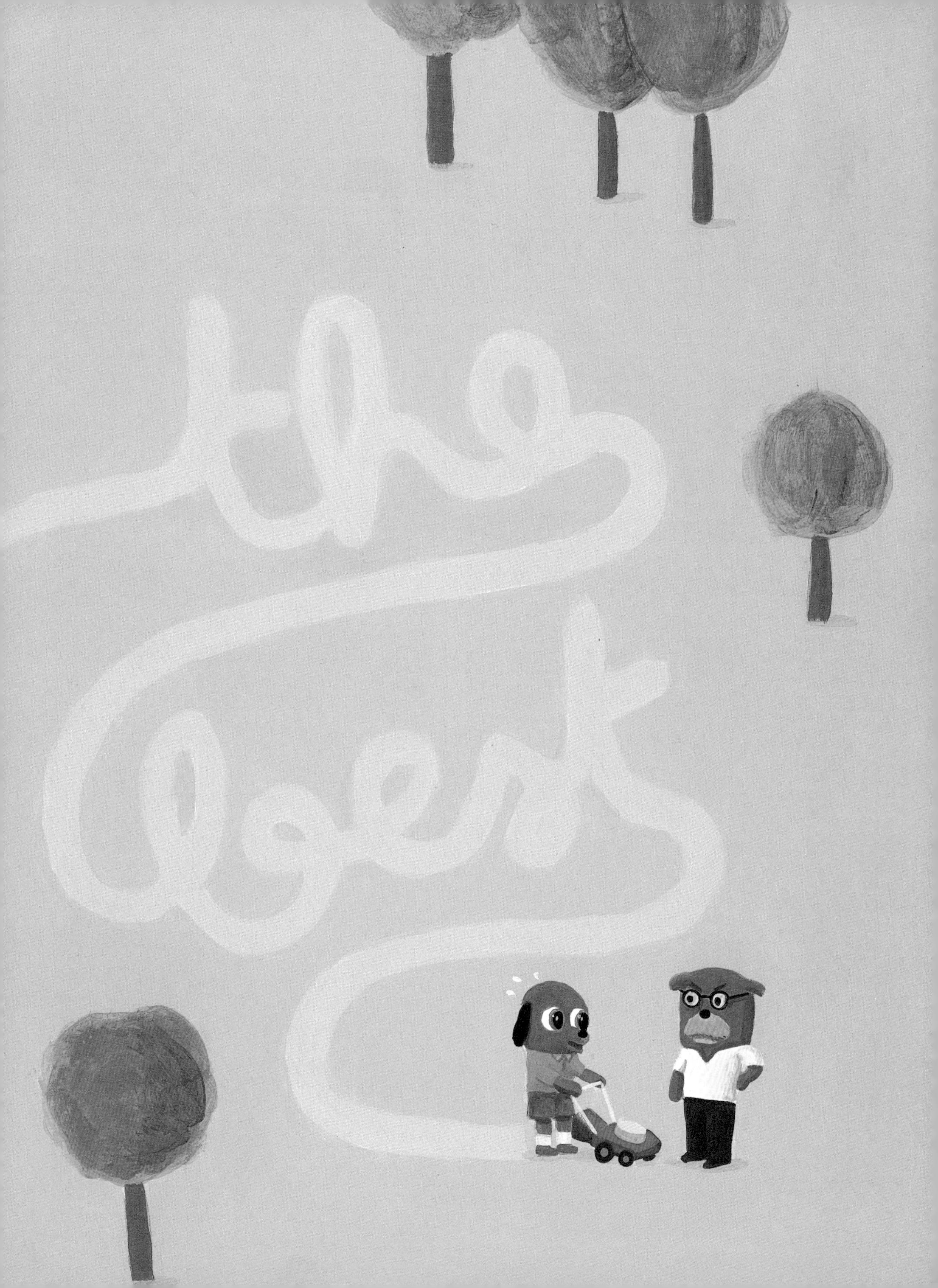
the best

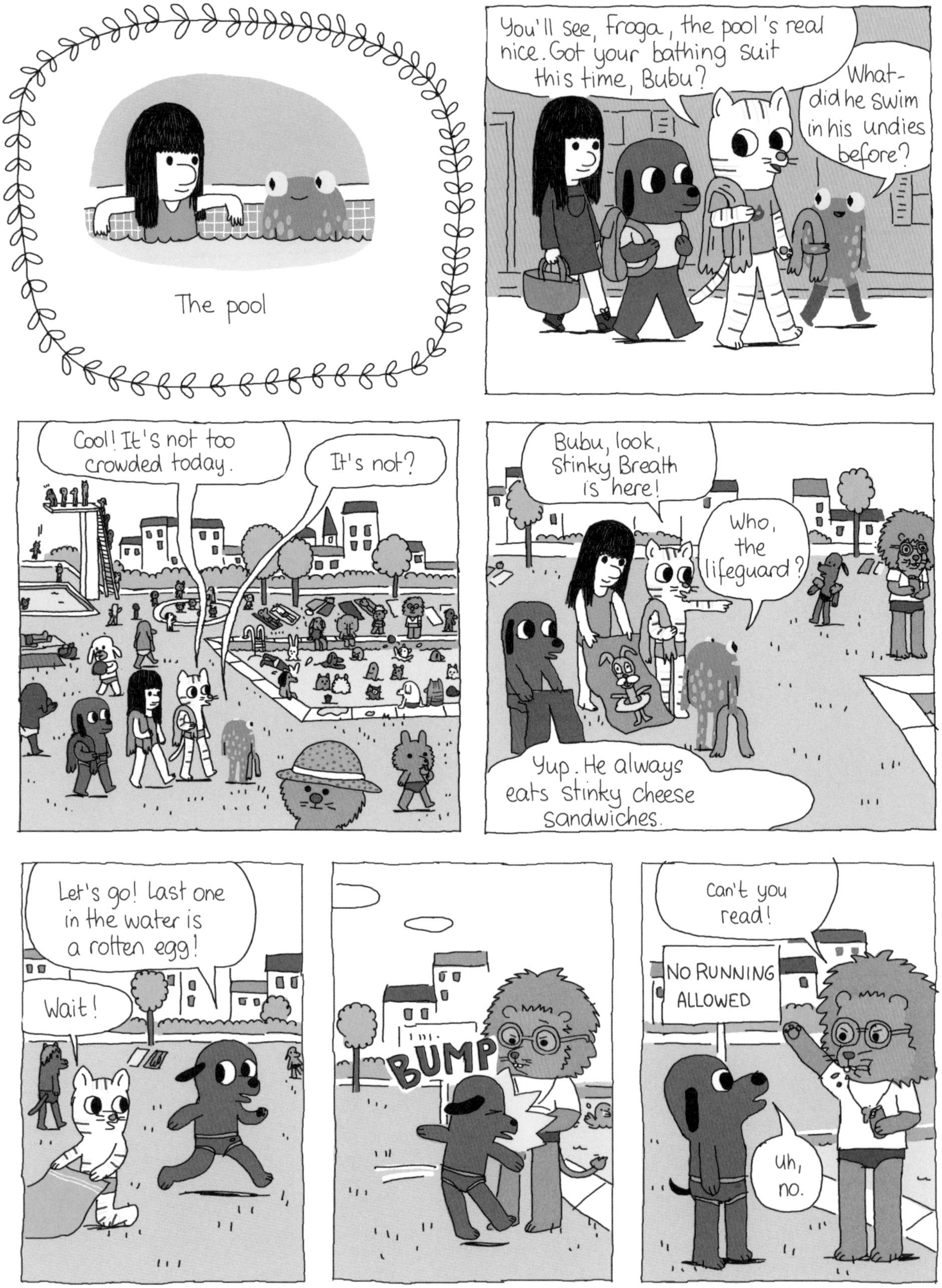
The pool
You'll see, Froga, the pool's real nice. Got your bathing suit this time, Bubu?
What-did he swim in his undies before?
Cool! It's not too crowded today.
It's not?
Bubu, look, Stinky Breath is here!
Who, the lifeguard?
Yup. He always eats stinky cheese sandwiches.
Let's go! Last one in the water is a rotten egg!
Wait!
BUMP
Can't you read!
NO RUNNING ALLOWED
Uh, no.

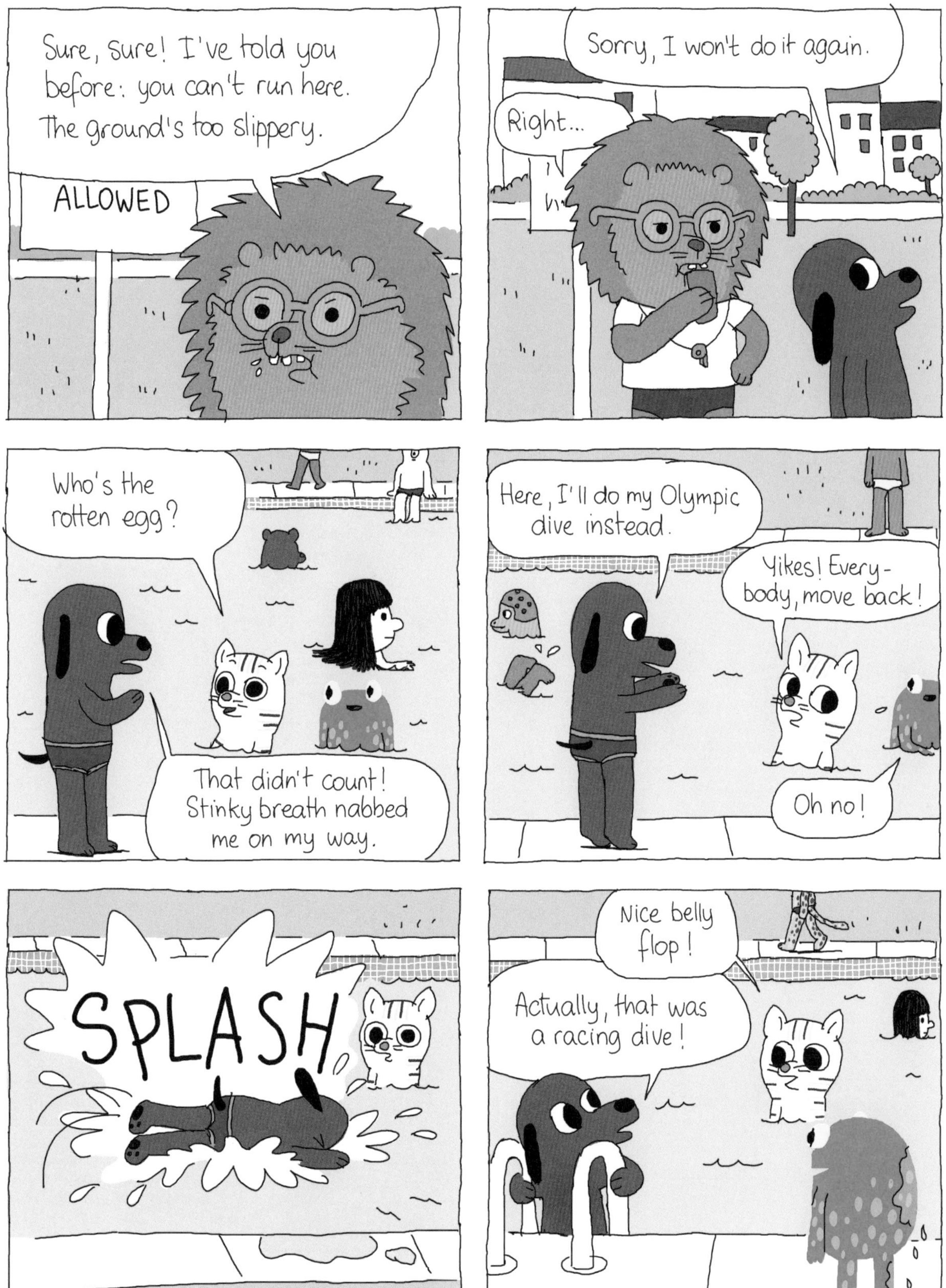
Sure, sure! I've told you before: you can't run here. The ground's too slippery.
ALLOWED
Sorry, I won't do it again.
Right...
Who's the rotten egg?
That didn't count! Stinky breath nabbed me on my way.
Here, I'll do my Olympic dive instead.
Yikes! Every-body, move back!
Oh no!
SPLASH
Nice belly flop!
Actually, that was a racing dive!

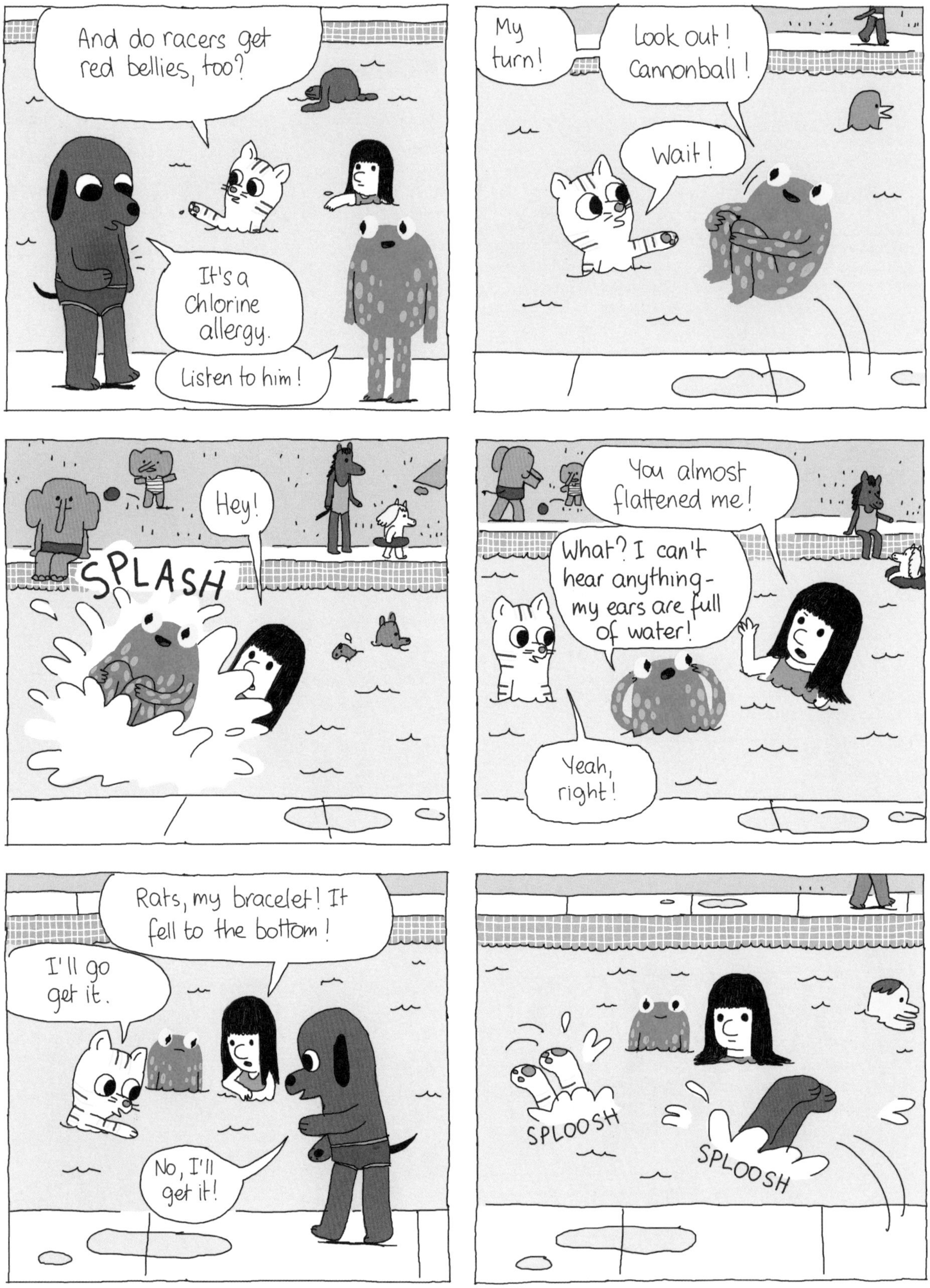

And do racers get red bellies, too?
It's a chlorine allergy.
Listen to him!
My turn!
Look out! Cannonball!
Wait!
Hey!
SPLASH
You almost flattened me!
What? I can't hear anything - my ears are full of water!
Yeah, right!
Rats, my bracelet! It fell to the bottom!
I'll go get it.
No, I'll get it!
SPLOOSH
SPLOOSH

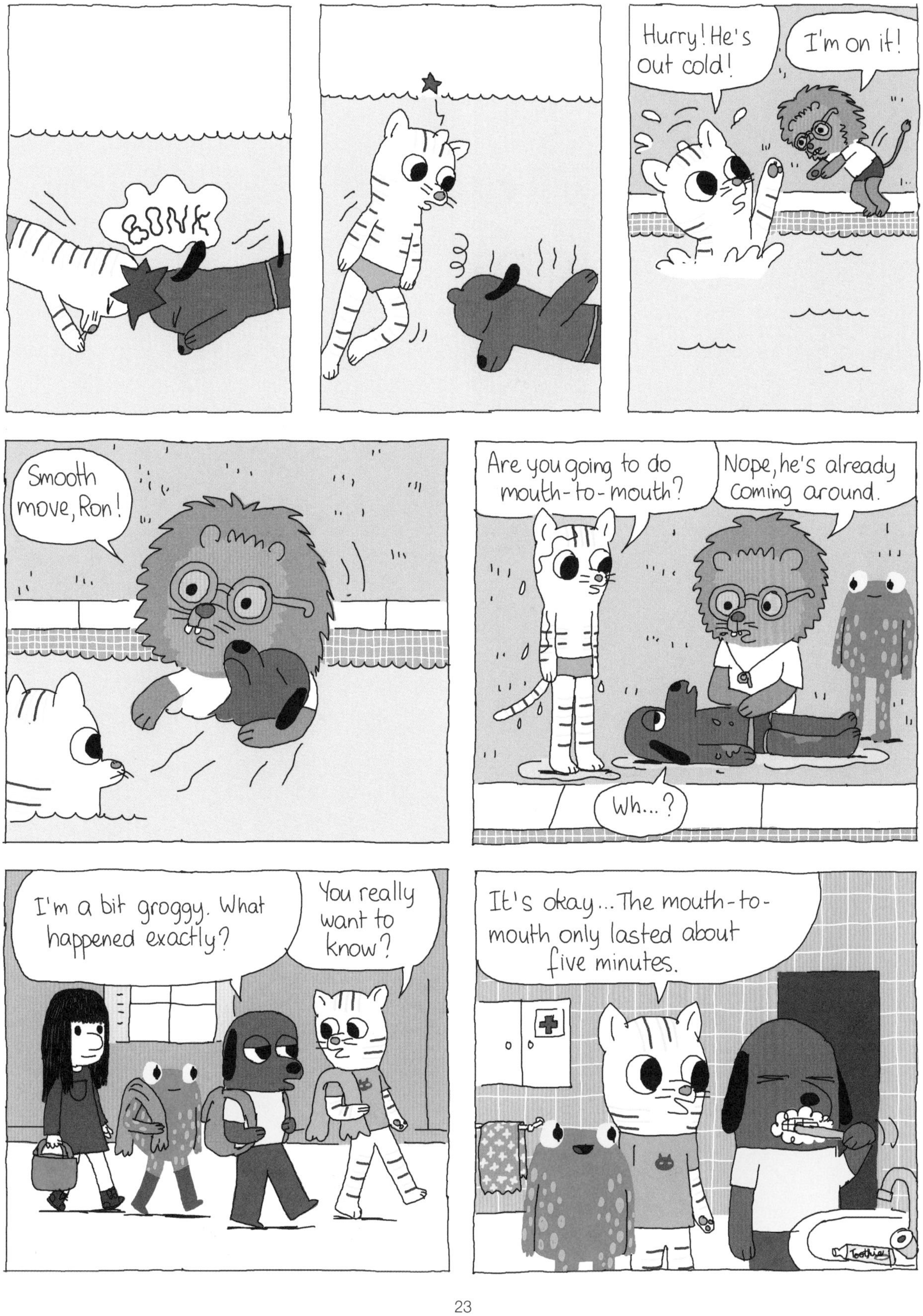
BONK
Hurry! He's out cold!
I'm on it!
Smooth move, Ron!
Are you going to do mouth-to-mouth?
Nope, he's already coming around.
Wh...?
I'm a bit groggy. What happened exactly?
You really want to know?
It's okay... The mouth-to-mouth only lasted about five minutes.
Toothie

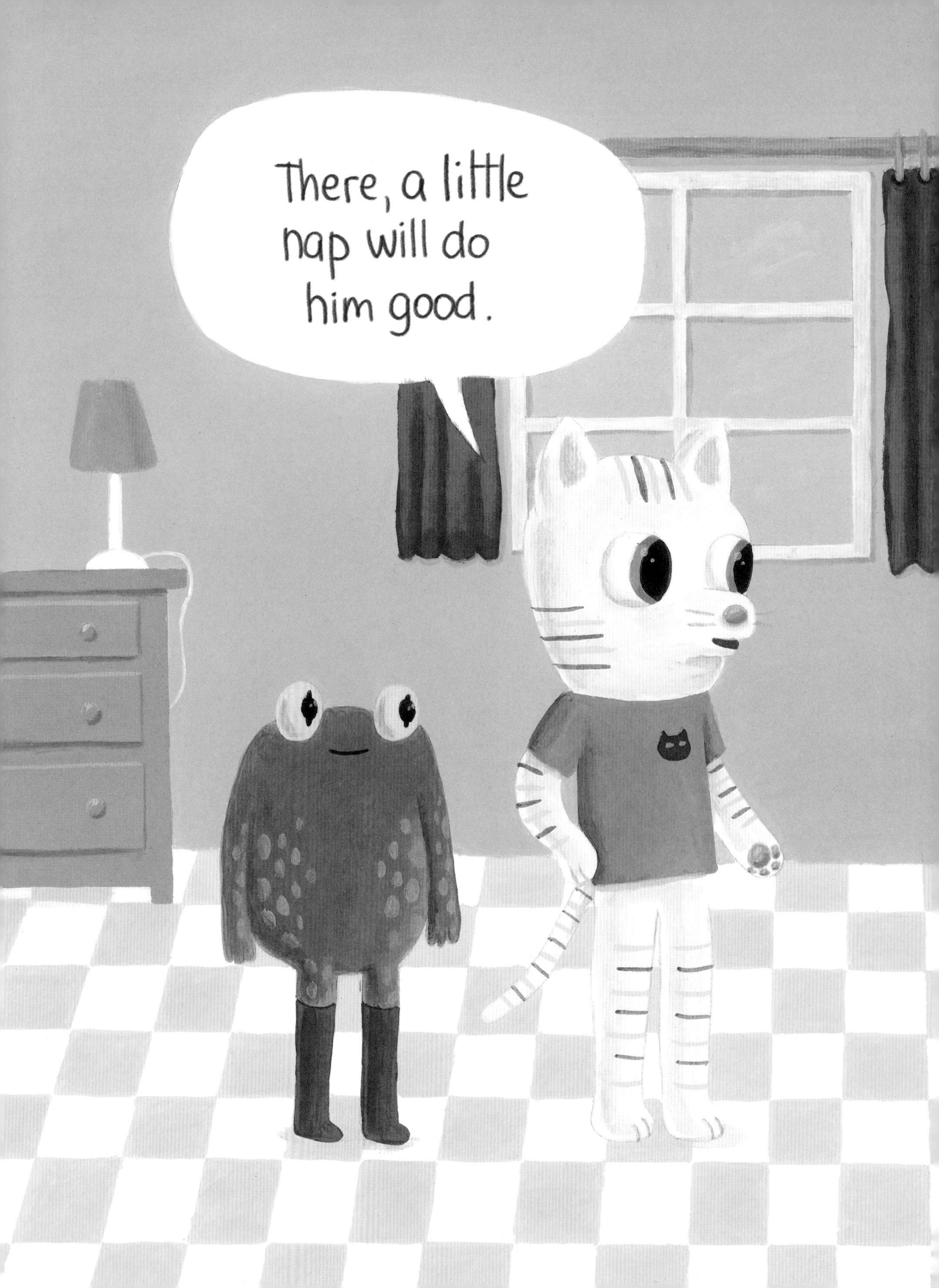
There, a little nap will do him good.

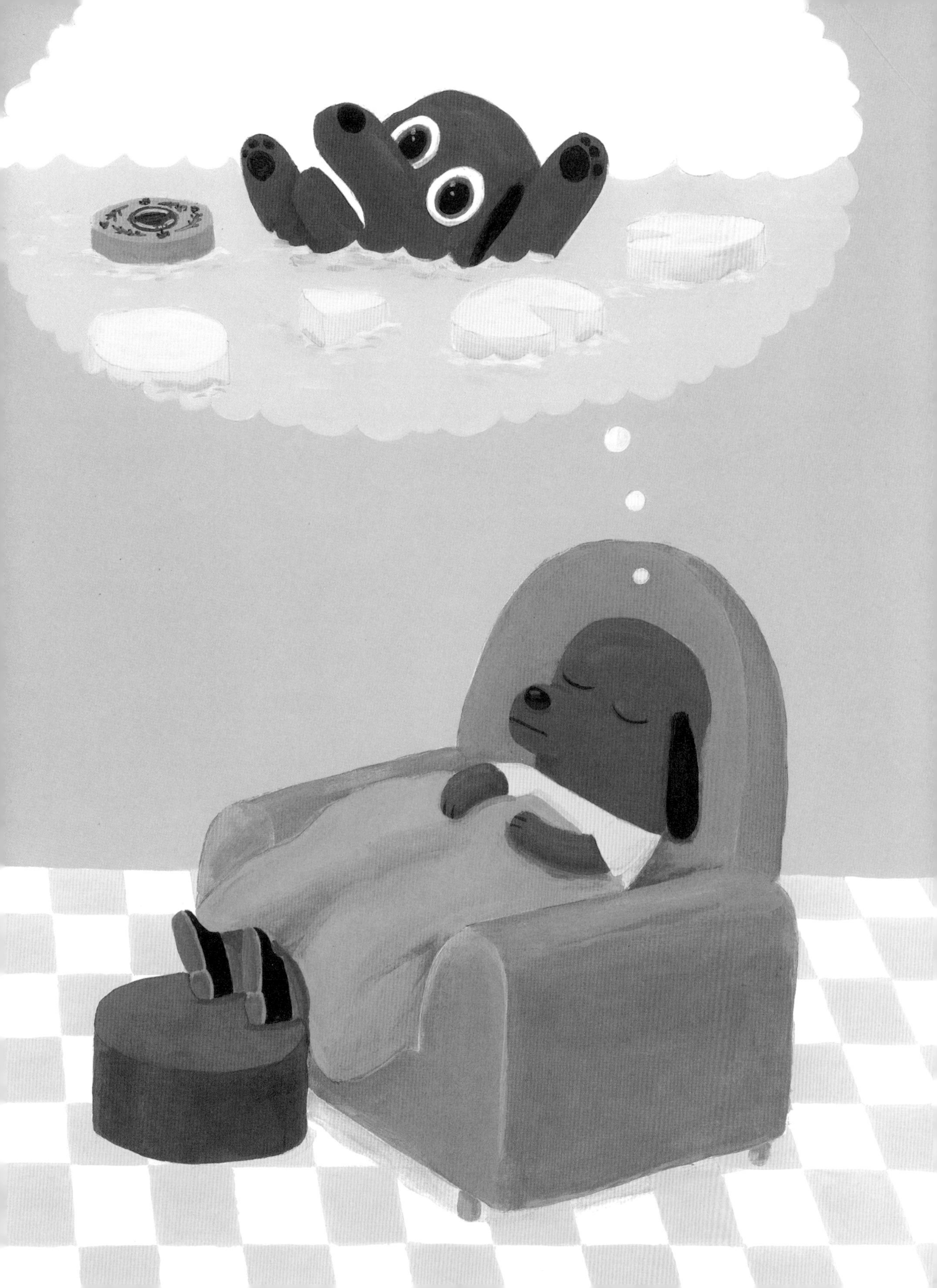

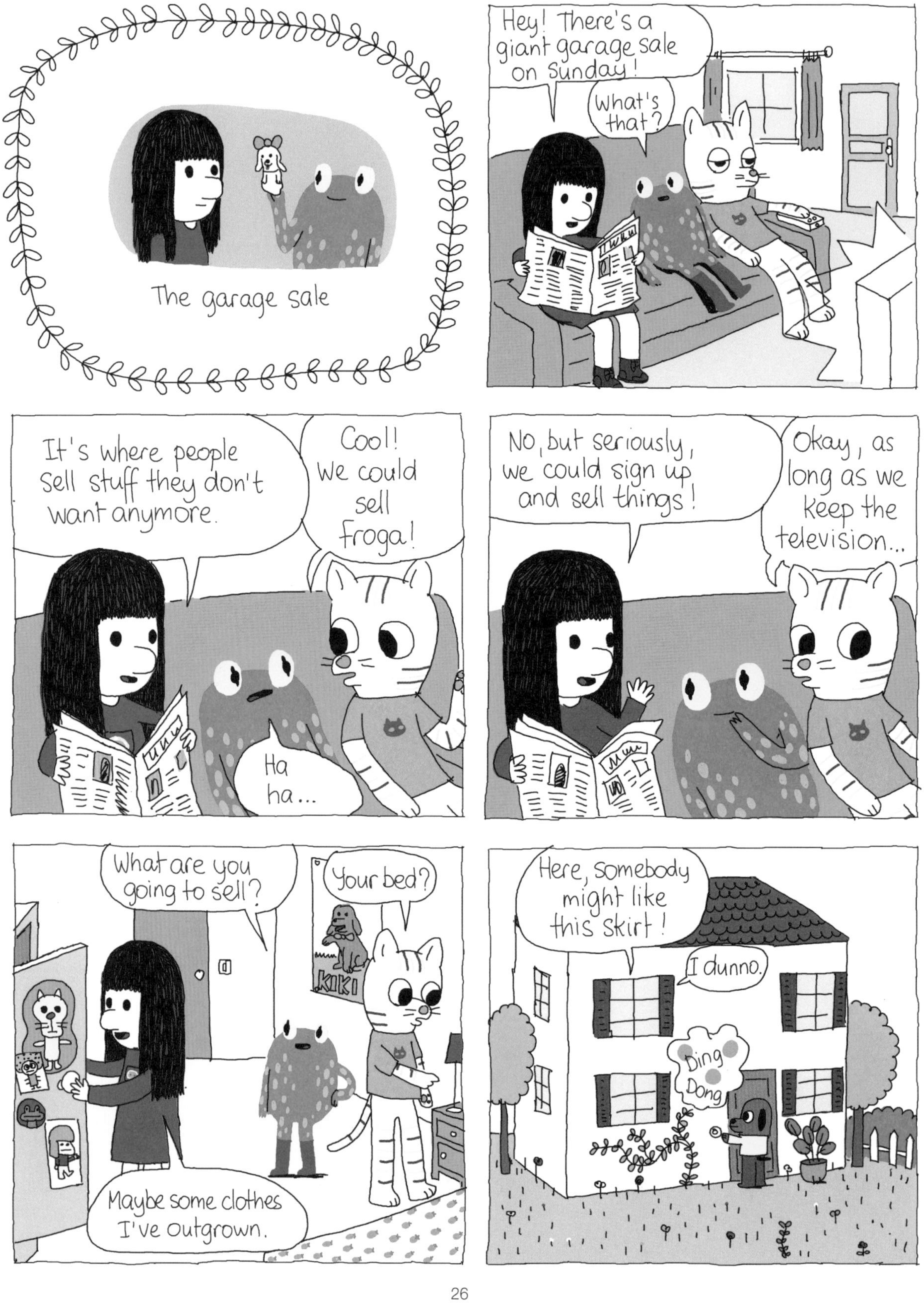

The garage sale
Hey! There's a giant garage sale on Sunday!
What's that?
It's where people sell stuff they don't want anymore.
Cool! We could sell Froga!
Ha ha...
No, but seriously, we could sign up and sell things!
Okay, as long as we keep the television...
What are you going to sell?
Your bed?
Maybe some clothes I've outgrown.
KIKI
Here, somebody might like this skirt!
I dunno.
Ding Dong

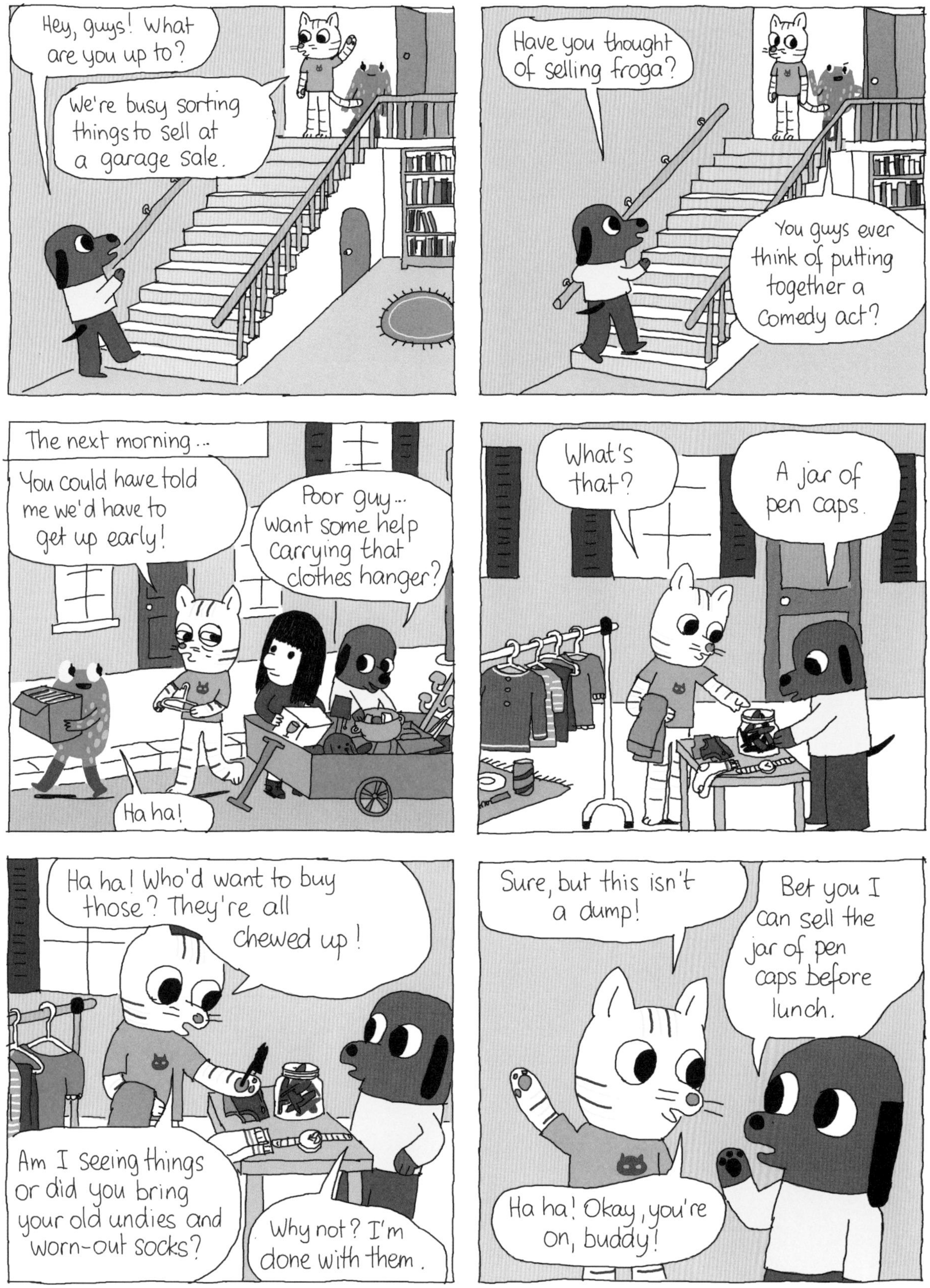
Hey, guys! What are you up to?
We're busy sorting things to sell at a garage sale.
Have you thought of selling froga?
You guys ever think of putting together a comedy act?
The next morning...
You could have told me we'd have to get up early!
Poor guy... want some help carrying that clothes hanger?
Ha ha!
What's that?
A jar of pen caps.
Ha ha! Who'd want to buy those? They're all chewed up!
Am I seeing things or did you bring your old undies and worn-out socks?
Why not? I'm done with them.
Sure, but this isn't a dump!
Bet you I can sell the jar of pen caps before lunch.
Ha ha! Okay, you're on, buddy!

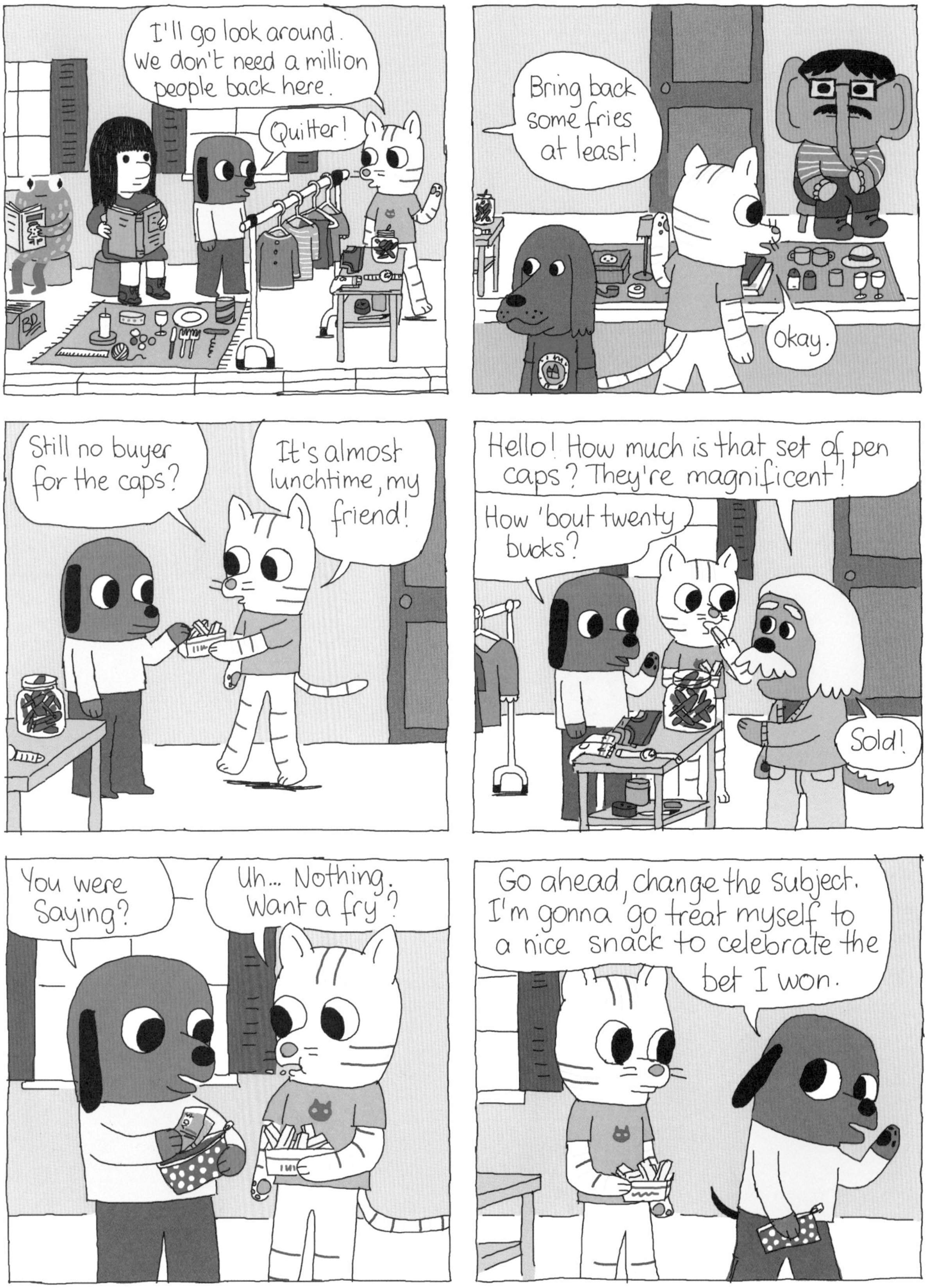
I'll go look around. We don't need a million people back here.
Quitter!
BD
Bring back some fries at least!
Okay.
Still no buyer for the caps?
It's almost lunchtime, my friend!
Hello! How much is that set of pen caps? They're magnificent!
How 'bout twenty bucks?
Sold!
You were saying?
Uh... Nothing. Want a fry?
Go ahead, change the subject. I'm gonna go treat myself to a nice snack to celebrate the bet I won.

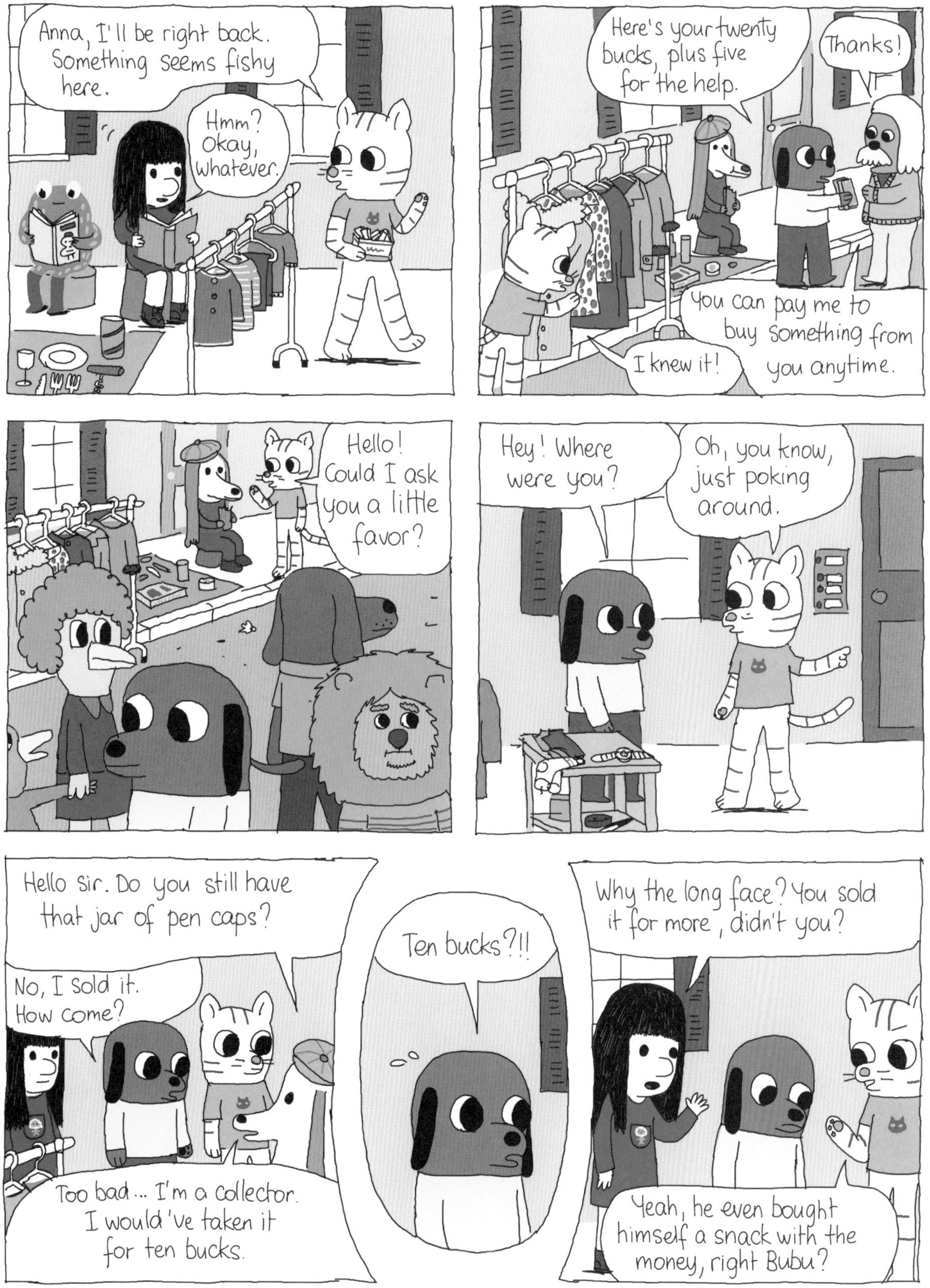
Anna, I'll be right back. Something seems fishy here.
Hmm? Okay, whatever.
Here's your twenty bucks, plus five for the help.
Thanks!
I knew it!
You can pay me to buy something from you anytime.
Hello! Could I ask you a little favor?
Hey! Where were you?
Oh, you know, just poking around.
Hello sir. Do you still have that jar of pen caps?
No, I sold it. How come?
Too bad... I'm a collector. I would've taken it for ten bucks.
Ten bucks?!!
Why the long face? You sold it for more, didn't you?
Yeah, he even bought himself a snack with the money, right Bubu?

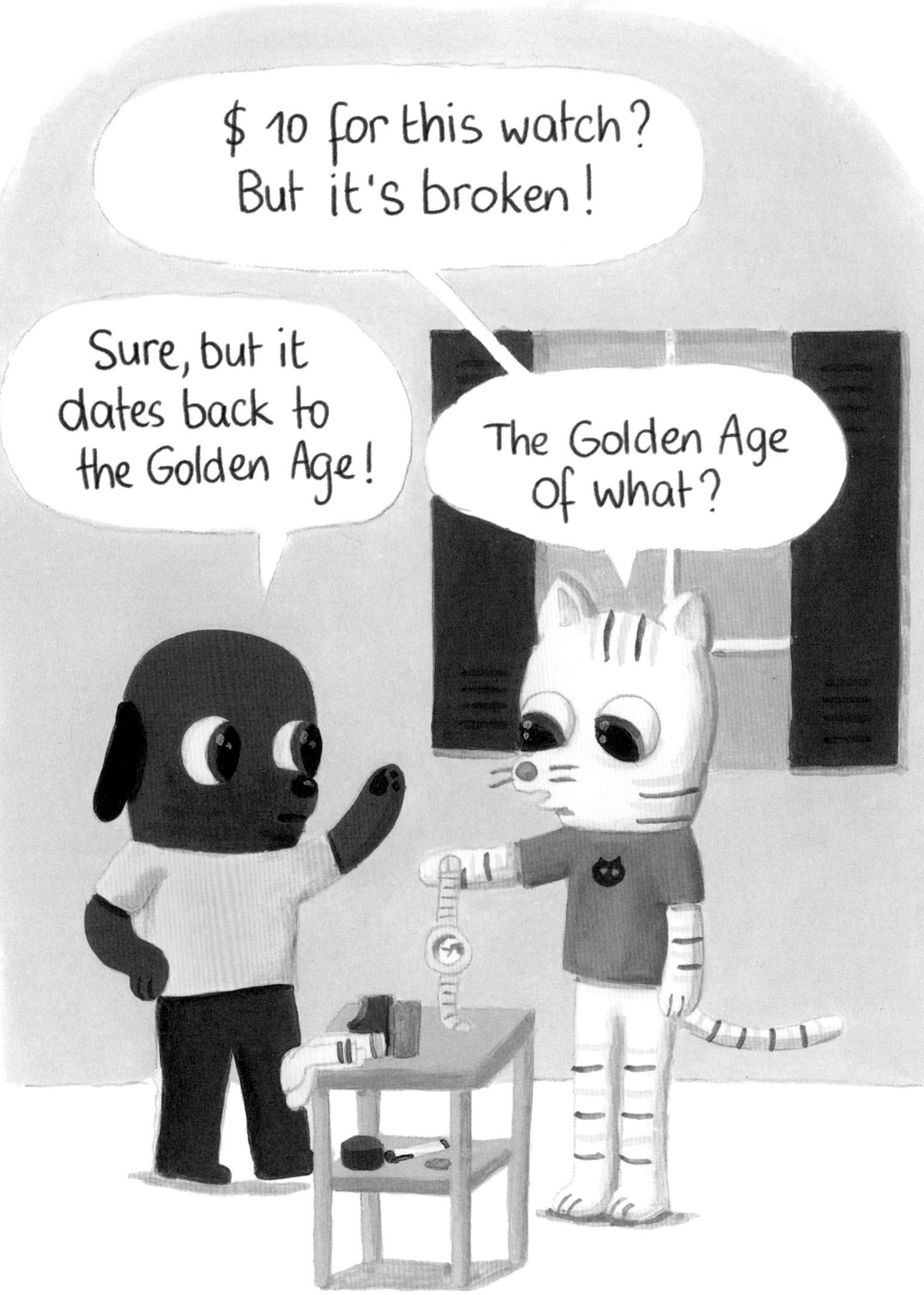
$ 10 for this watch? But it's broken!
Sure, but it dates back to the Golden Age!
The Golden Age of what?

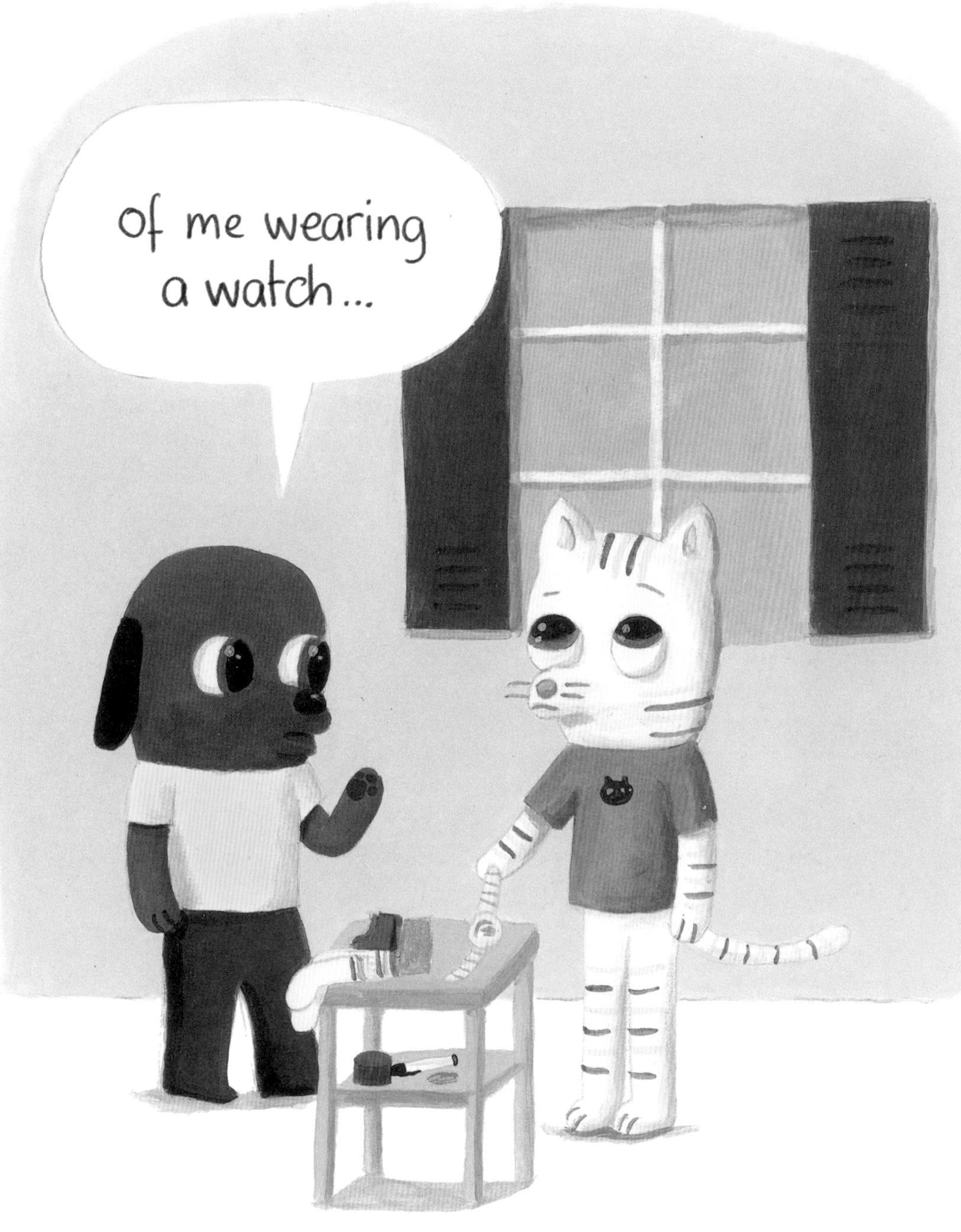
of me wearing a watch...

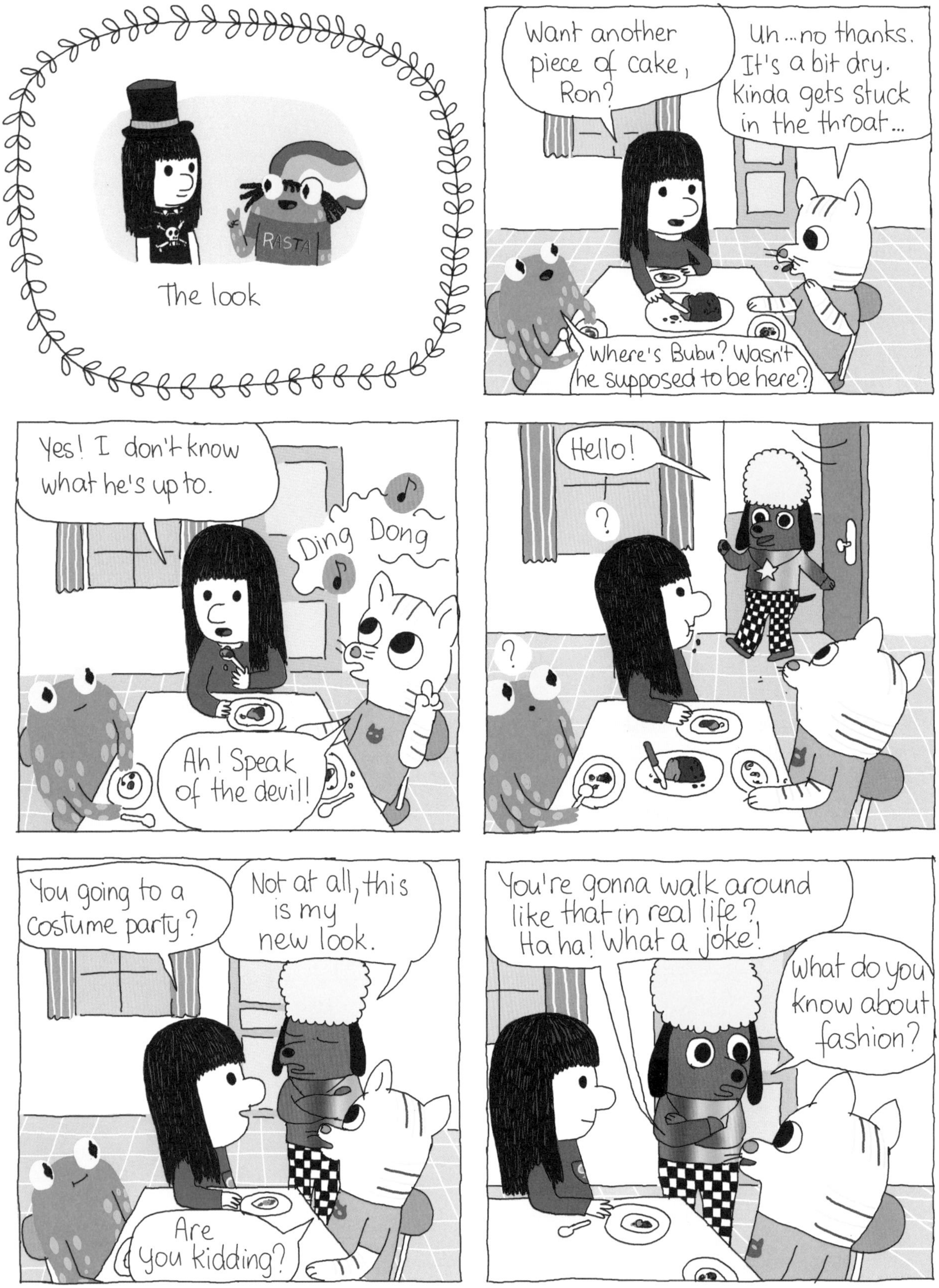
The look
Want another piece of cake, Ron?
Uh ...no thanks. It's a bit dry. Kinda gets stuck in the throat...
Where's Bubu? Wasn't he supposed to be here?
Yes! I don't know what he's up to.
Ding Dong
Ah! Speak of the devil!
Hello!
?
?
You going to a costume party?
Not at all, this is my new look.
Are you kidding?
You're gonna walk around like that in real life? Ha ha! What a joke!
What do you know about fashion?

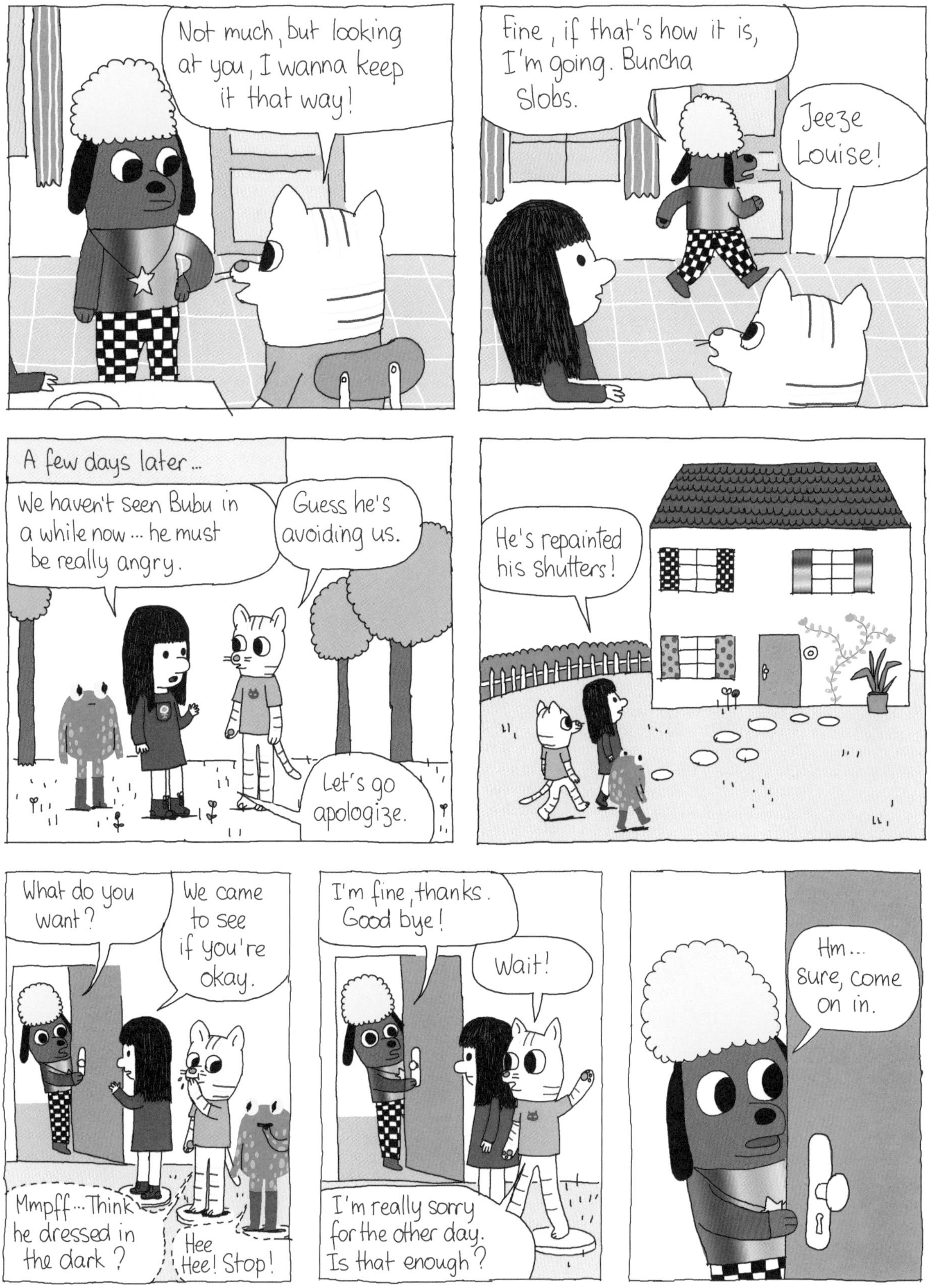
Not much, but looking at you, I wanna keep it that way!
Fine, if that's how it is, I'm going. Buncha Slobs.
Jeeze Louise!
A few days later...
We haven't seen Bubu in a while now... he must be really angry.
Guess he's avoiding us.
Let's go apologize.
He's repainted his shutters!
What do you want?
We came to see if you're okay.
Mmpff... Think he dressed in the dark?
Hee Hee! Stop!
I'm fine, thanks. Good bye!
Wait!
I'm really sorry for the other day. Is that enough?
Hm... sure, come on in.

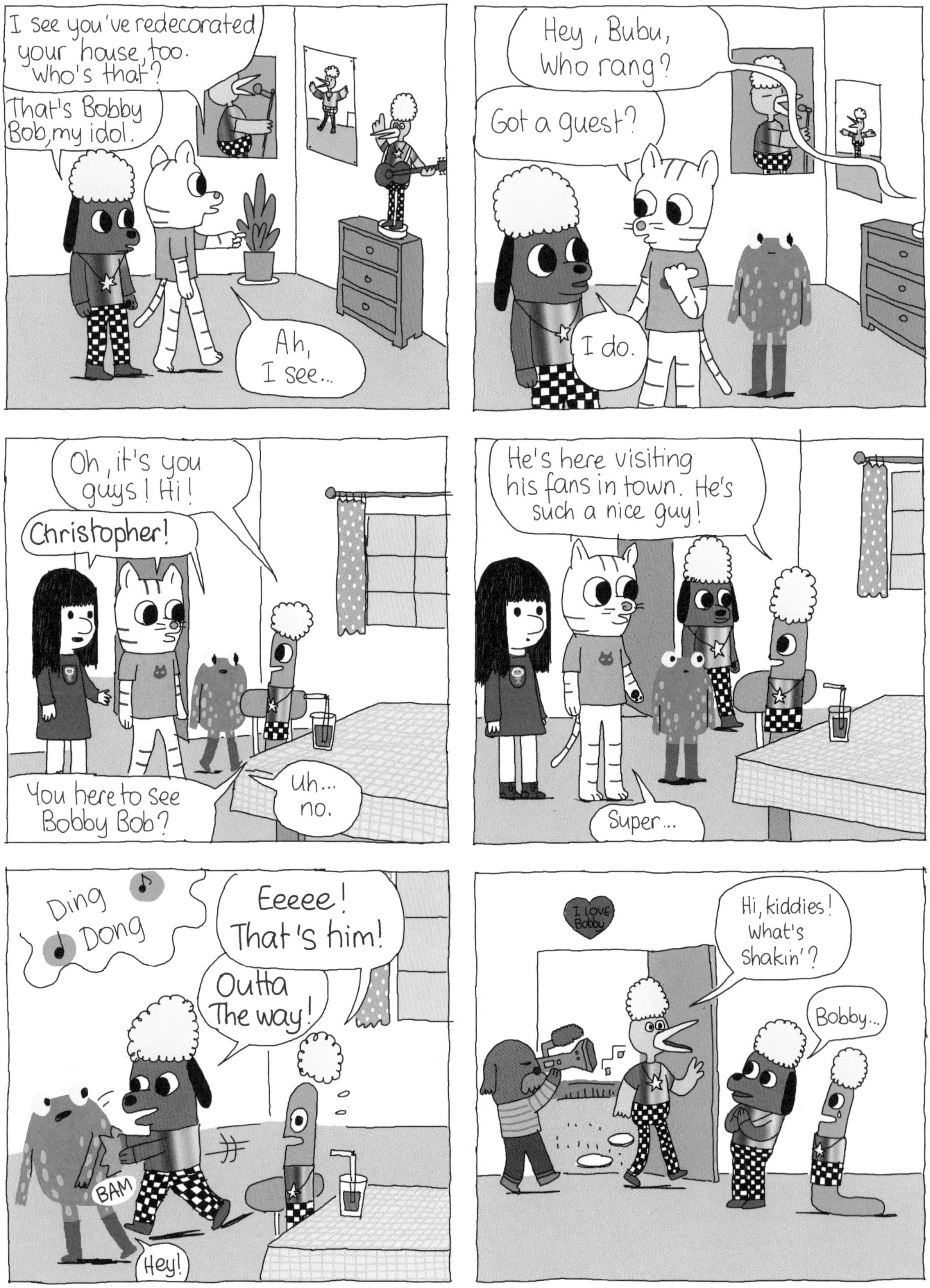
I see you've redecorated your house, too. Who's that?
That's Bobby Bob, my idol.
Ah, I see...
Hey, Bubu, Who rang?
Got a guest?
I do.
Oh, it's you guys! Hi!
Christopher!
You here to see Bobby Bob?
Uh... no.
He's here visiting his fans in town. He's such a nice guy!
Super...
Ding Dong
Eeeee! That's him!
Outta The way!
BAM
Hey!
I LOVE Bobby
Hi, kiddies! What's Shakin'?
Bobby...

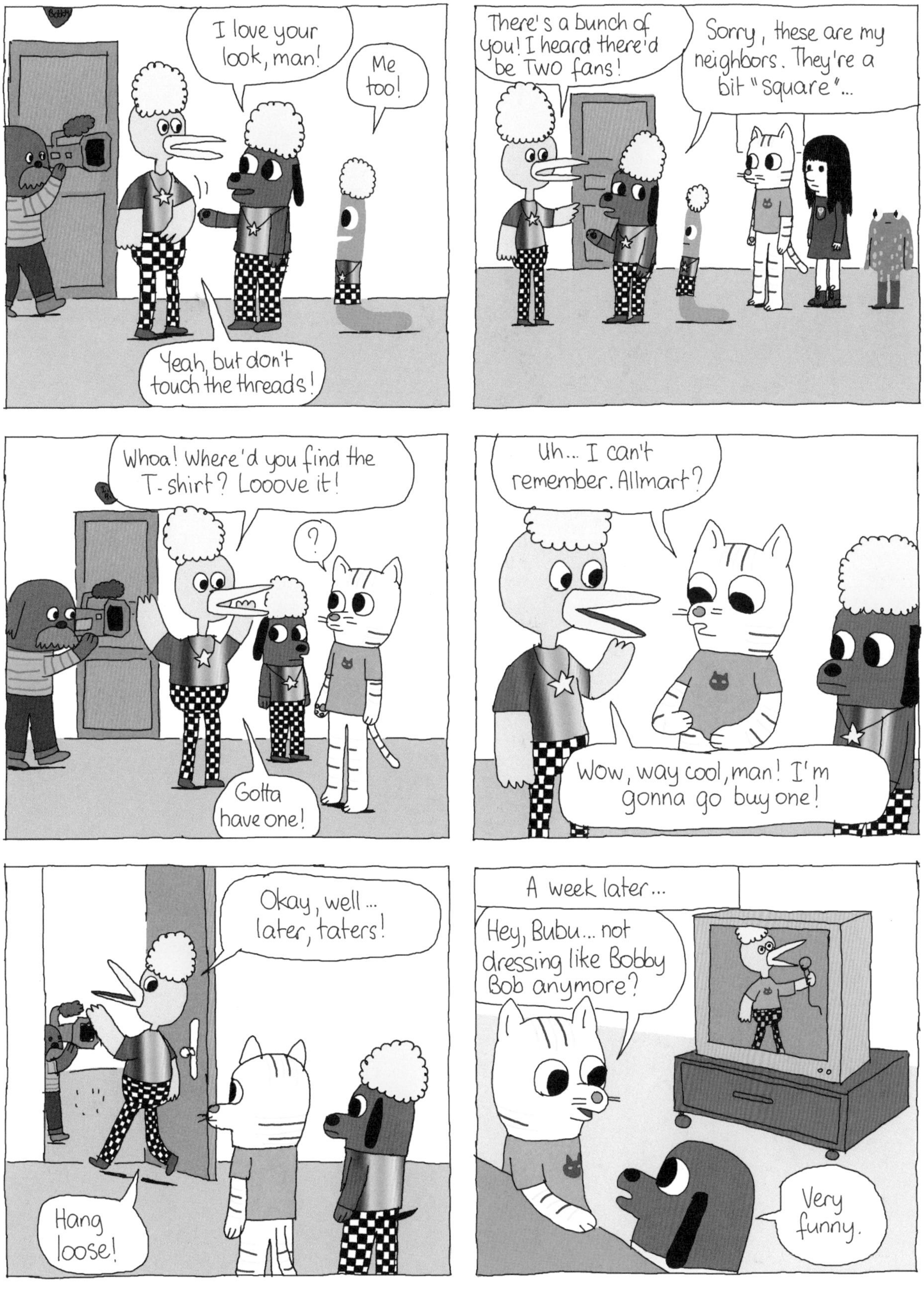

I love your look, man!
Me too!
Yeah, but don't touch the threads!
There's a bunch of you! I heard there'd be TWO fans!
Sorry, these are my neighbors. They're a bit "square"...
Whoa! Where'd you find the T-shirt? Looove it!
?
Gotta have one!
Uh... I can't remember. Allmart?
Wow, way cool, man! I'm gonna go buy one!
Okay, well... later, taters!
Hang loose!
A week later...
Hey, Bubu... not dressing like Bobby Bob anymore?
Very funny.

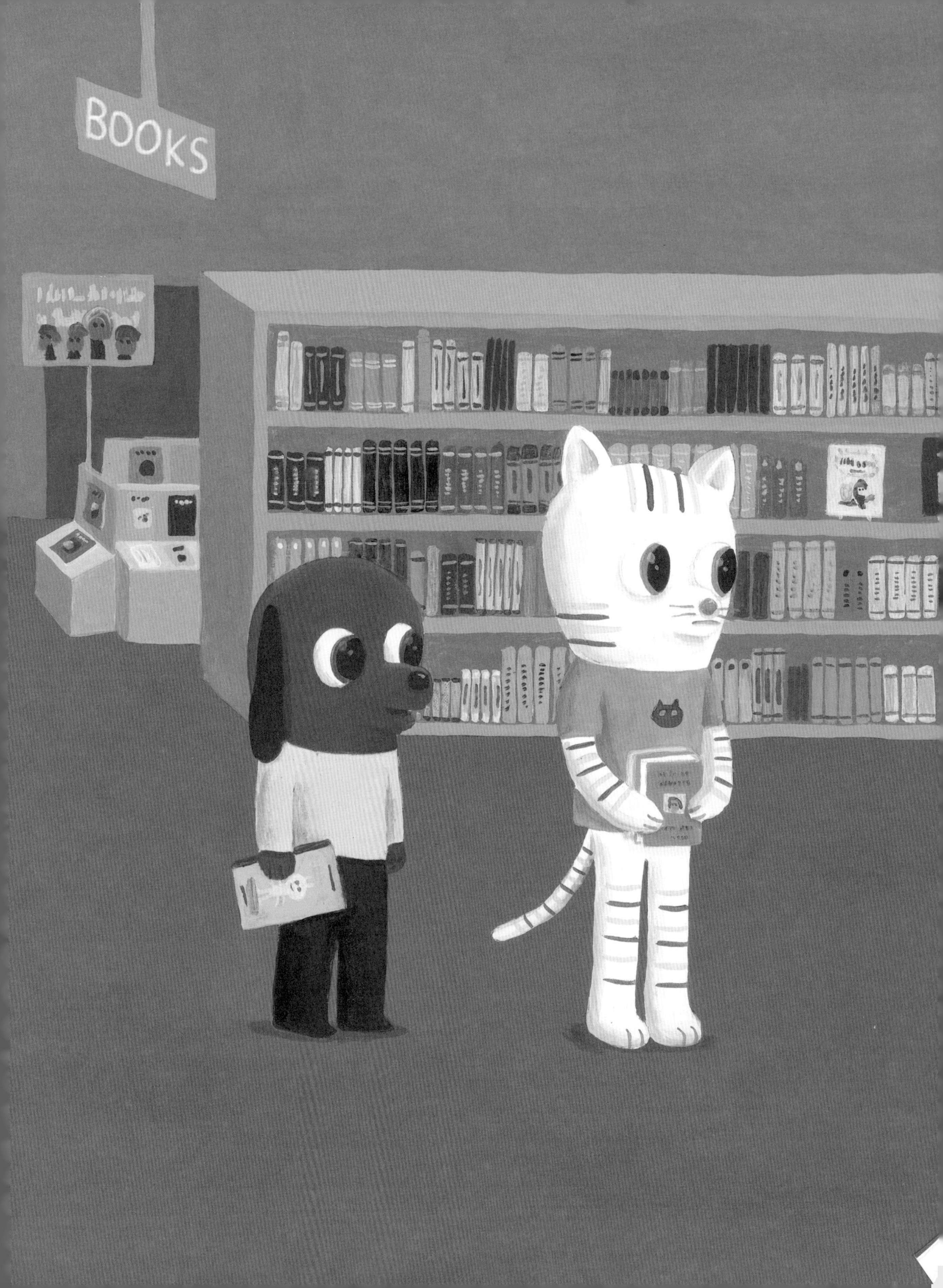
BOOKS

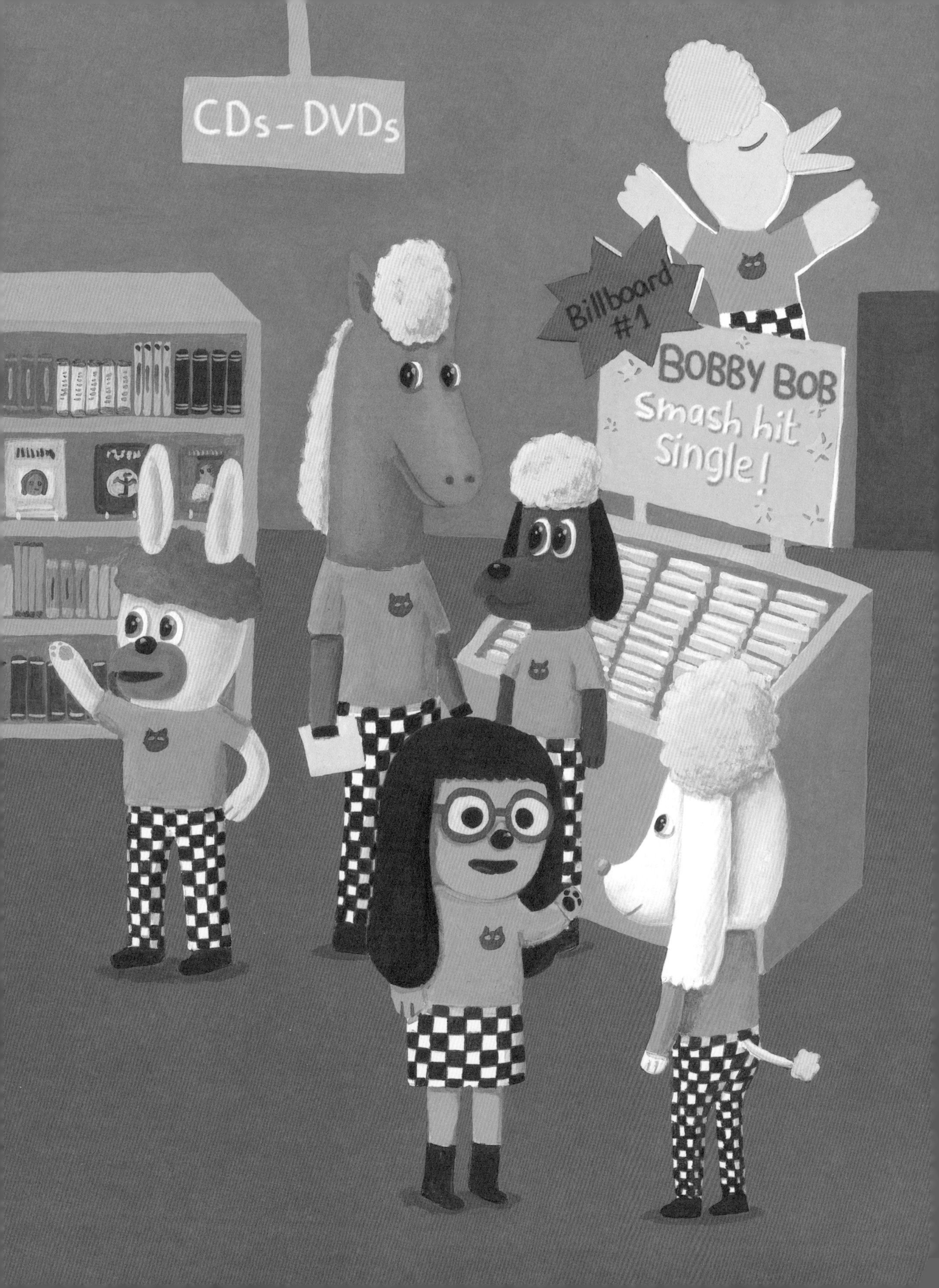
CDs - DVDs
Billboard #1
BOBBY BOB
Smash hit
Single!

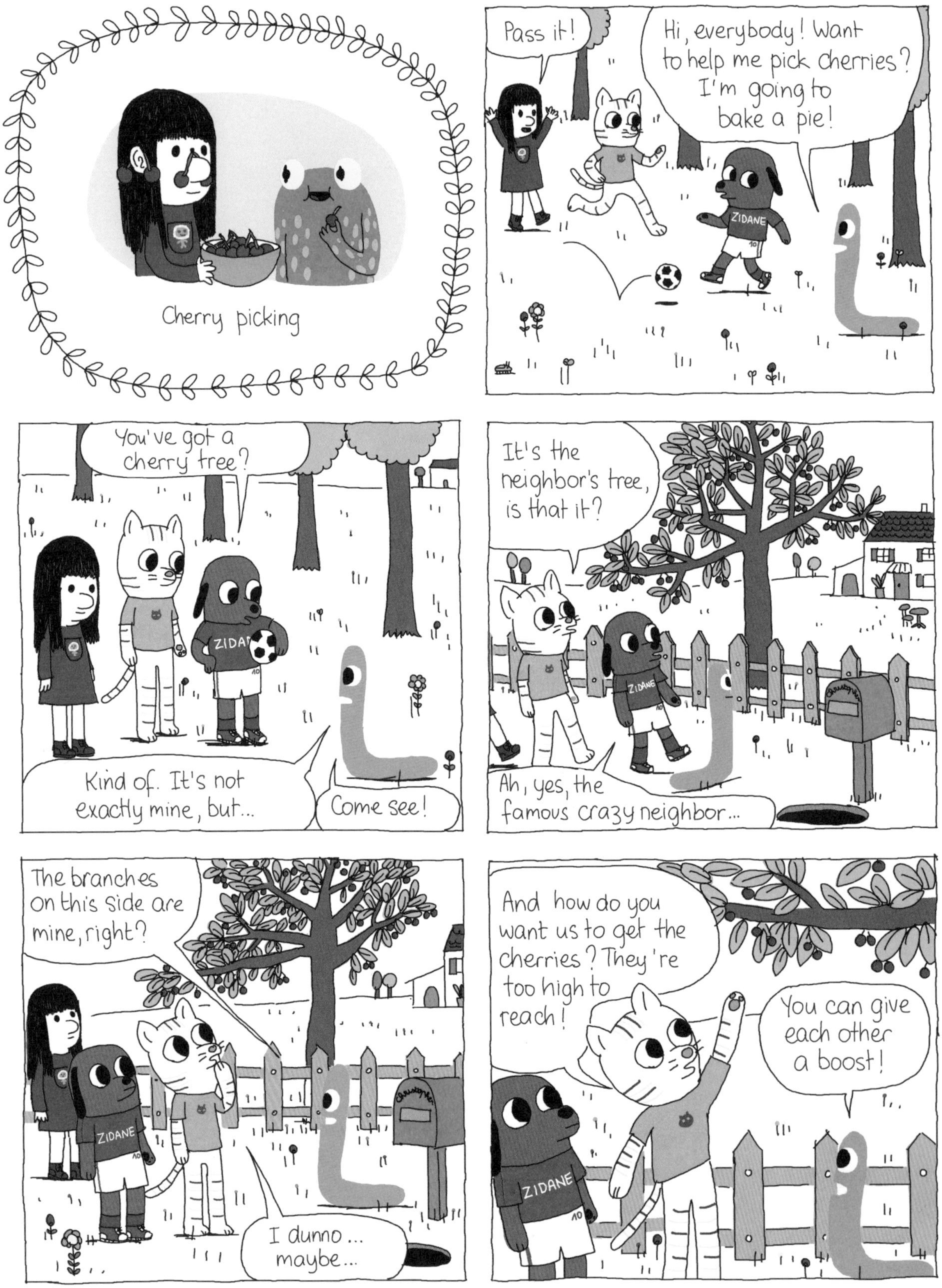
Cherry picking
Pass it!
Hi, everybody! Want to help me pick cherries? I'm going to bake a pie!
ZIDANE
You've got a cherry tree?
Kind of. It's not exactly mine, but...
Come see!
It's the neighbor's tree, is that it?
Ah, yes, the famous crazy neighbor...
The branches on this side are mine, right?
I dunno... maybe...
And how do you want us to get the cherries? They're too high to reach!
You can give each other a boost!

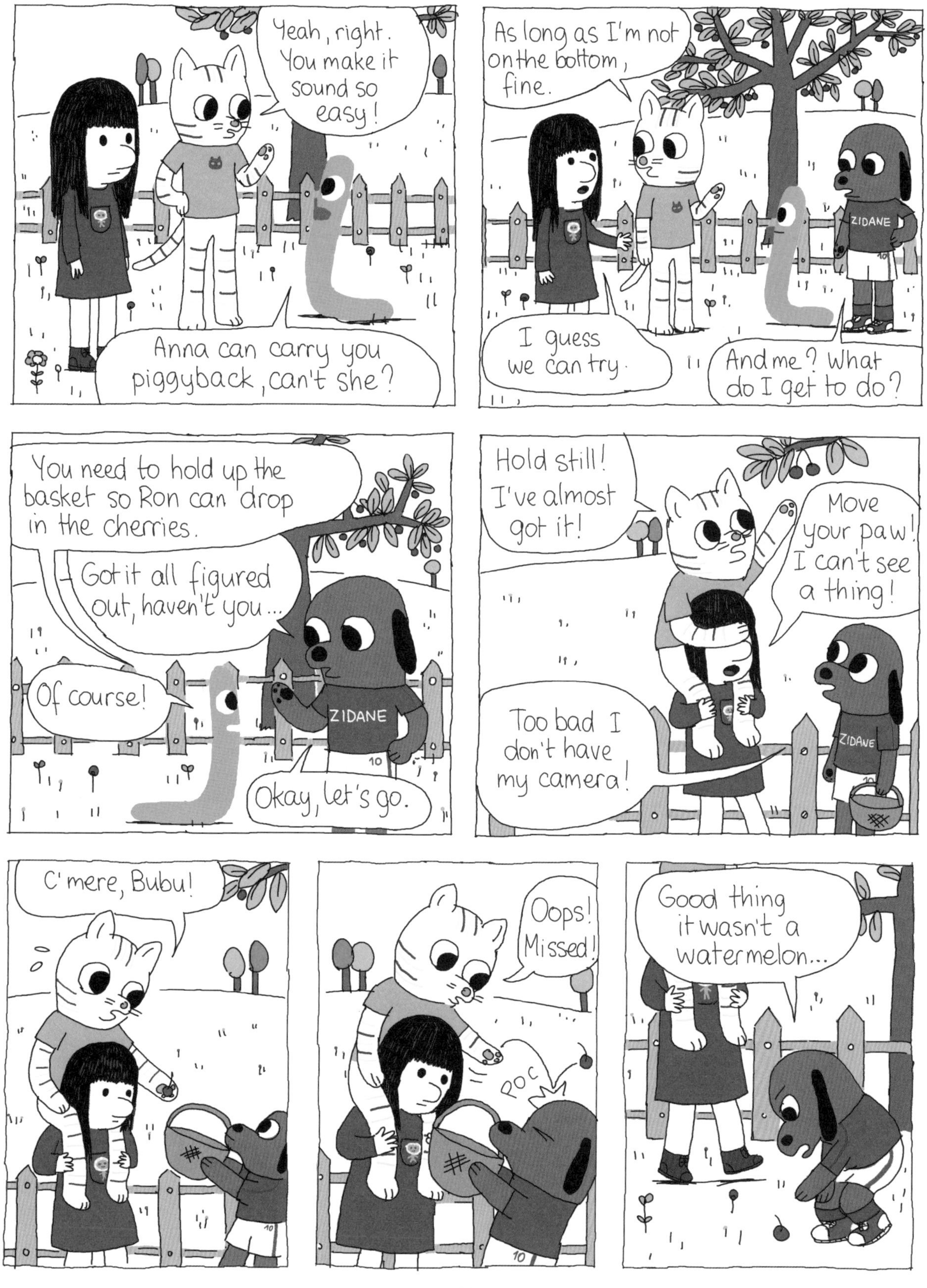
Yeah, right. You make it sound so easy!
Anna can carry you piggyback, can't she?
As long as I'm not on the bottom, fine.
I guess we can try.
And me? What do I get to do?
ZIDANE
You need to hold up the basket so Ron can drop in the cherries.
Got it all figured out, haven't you...
Of course!
ZIDANE
Okay, let's go.
Hold still! I've almost got it!
Move your paw! I can't see a thing!
Too bad I don't have my camera!
ZIDANE
C'mere, Bubu!
Oops! Missed!
POC
Good thing it wasn't a watermelon...

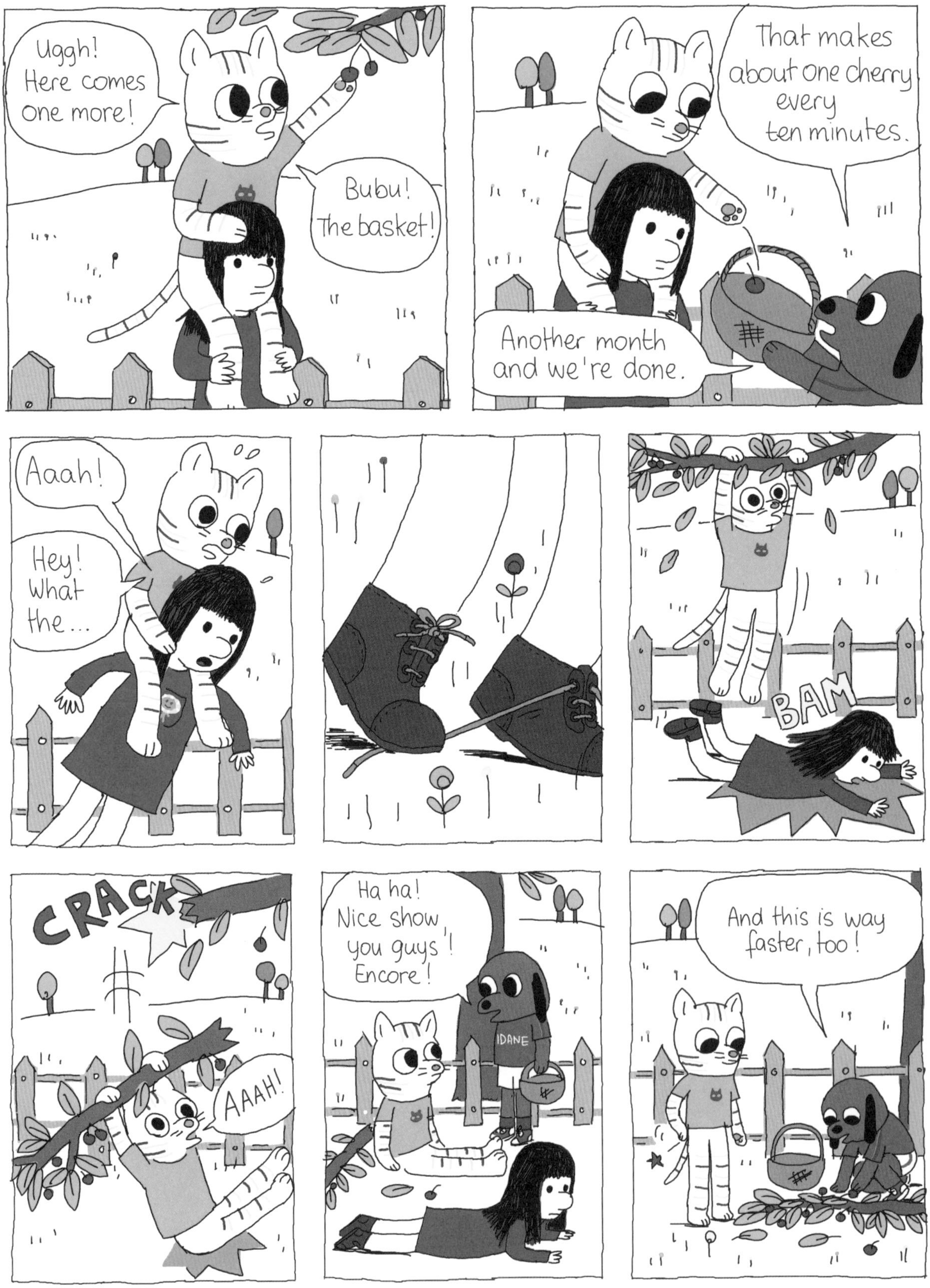
Uggh! Here comes one more!
Bubu! The basket!
That makes about one cherry every ten minutes.
Another month and we're done.
Aaah!
Hey! What the...
BAM
CRACK
AAAH!
Ha ha! Nice show you guys! Encore!
IDANE
And this is way faster, too!

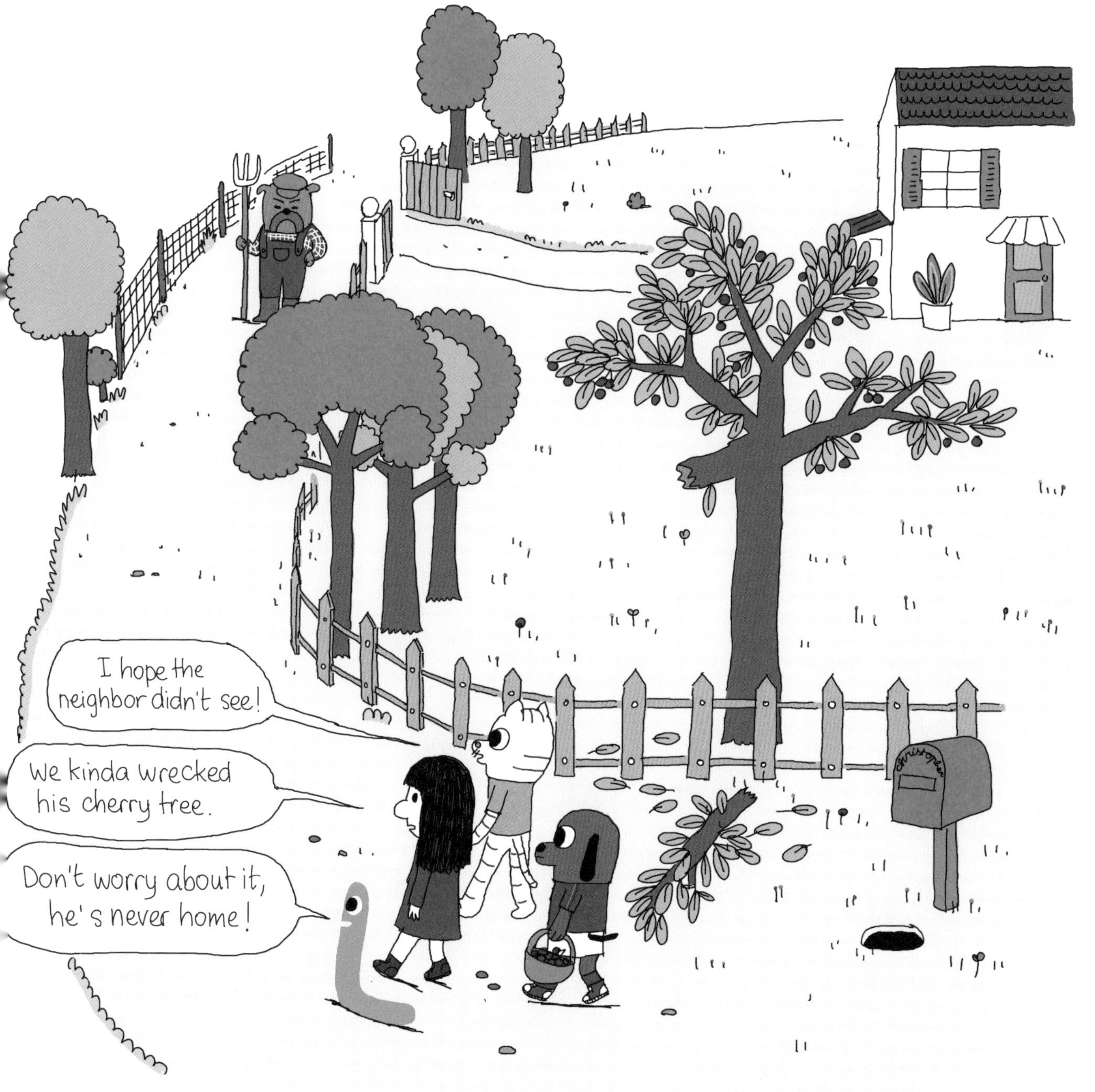
I hope the neighbor didn't see!
We kinda wrecked his cherry tree.
Don't worry about it, he's never home!